Scouting for the Reaper

Scouting for the Reaper

Stories

Jacob M. Appel

www.blacklawrence.com

Executive Editor: Diane Goettel
Cover and book design: Amy Freels

ISBN: 978-1-937854-95-9

Published 2014 by Black Lawrence Press
Printed in the United States

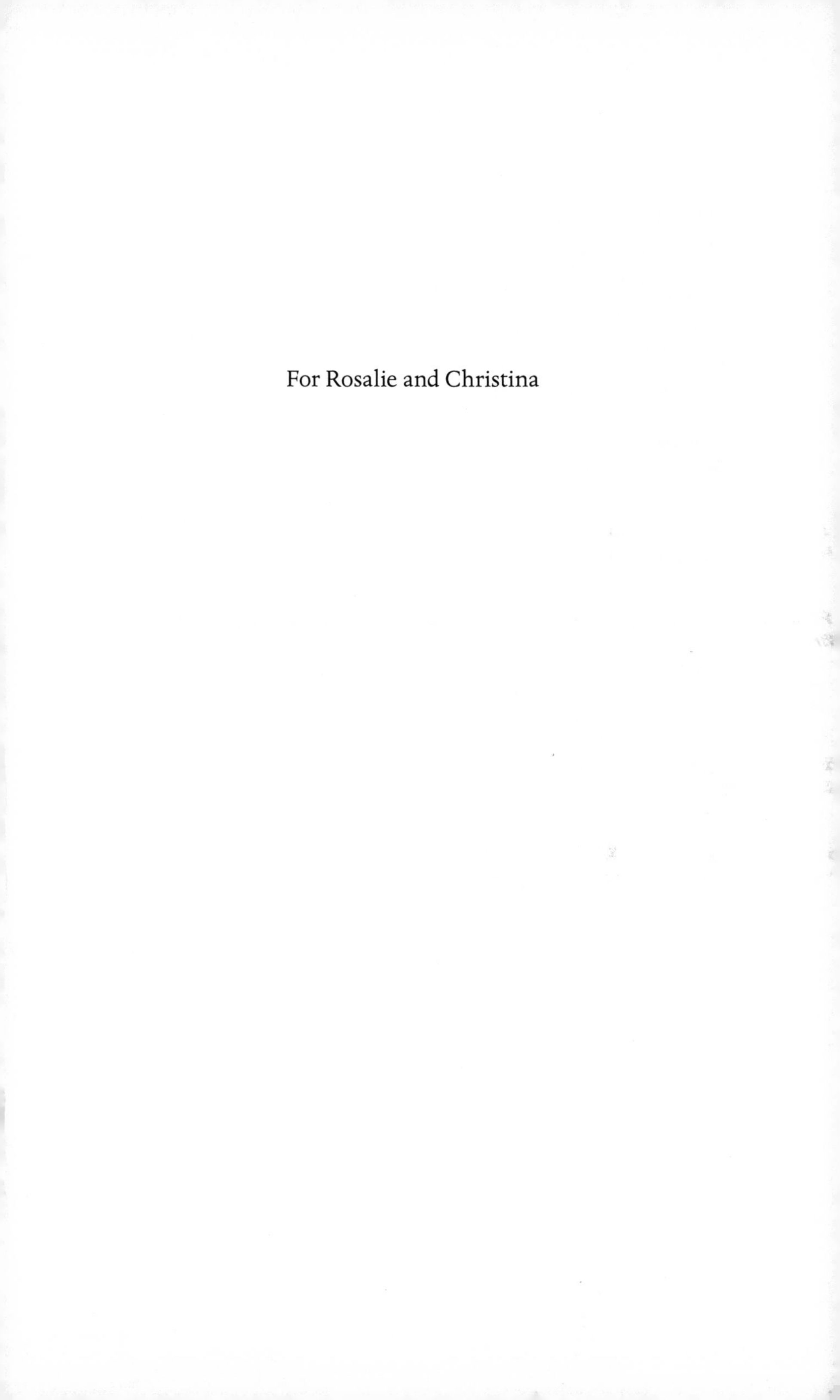

For Rosalie and Christina

Contents

Choose Your Own Genetics

Miss Stanley was new to the ninth grade that autumn, and we could all sense that she wasn't cut out for it. She was twenty-three years old and had been hired as a last-minute replacement for Mrs. Tubbs, an overweight black woman who'd shattered her pelvis in an escalator accident. "We're going to learn the ropes together," Miss Stanley explained that first morning, "so if you have any ideas for improving class, you shouldn't be afraid to share them. Science is all about experimentation." After that, she wrote her lesson plan on the chalkboard and checked off each item as we completed it:

I. Laboratory Rules.
II. Why Biology is Exciting.
III. Personal Introductions.
IV. Historical Examples.
V. Homework.

To explain why biology was exciting, she read aloud for twenty minutes from the opening pages of Darwin's *On the Origin of Species*. When the opportunity finally arrived for personal introductions, Miss Stanley confessed that she would be at Commodore Perry for only one year, while she applied to veterinary schools. She thought teaching would be a "rewarding" way to use her "year off." I introduced myself as Natalie—my middle name, although up until then I'd always gone by Louise. I explained how I'd spent my summer shadowing a grad student at Brown University, where my father ran the Genetics Department. Next, Jonah Driscoll told the class that he'd spent his summer studying Irish whiskey at Sullivan's Saloon, where his mother waited tables. Miss Stanley did not smile, but I did. For me, Jonah's voice—deep and cavalier—was as intoxicating as Sullivan's liquor. Then Shorty Foust asked how Mrs. Tubbs had *really* broken her pelvis.

"Please, enough," said Miss Stanley, turning her slender wrist inward to glance at the platinum sliver of her watch. "Let's not get distracted."

She took a deep breath, as though she might be counting to ten inside her head, and I could swear I saw a tear glint in the crook of her eye. That was the first and last time I ever felt bad for her. Not because she was floundering, but because she looked so incredibly lonely. Georgia Stanley, big-boned, not pretty, probably a virgin at twenty-three, was the woman I could so easily become—except I was smart. "We'll do the rest of the introductions tomorrow," she announced, placing a "+/-" alongside *III. Personal Introductions.* "Now I want to talk about how biology can shape history. Who can name the U.S. President who suffered from an infectious disease?"

A drowsy silence fell over the room. Miss Stanley paced between the desks, like a talk show host, her legs far too chunky for her high-cut skirt. I didn't mind how long the class dragged on. I was thankful for each minute in the same room with Jonah.

"This isn't a hard question," said Miss Stanley, sounding more disappointed than frustrated. "You've all studied history, haven't you?"

Shorty Foust muttered, "I bet Bill Clinton caught something from Monica."

Some of the other boys laughed nervously, but not Jonah.

"Franklin Roosevelt is the answer," said Miss Stanley. "FDR couldn't walk because he'd had the polio virus in his thirties. . . . Now how about a genetic disease? This is a harder one. Which U.S. President most likely had a genetic disorder?"

My dad had already taught me about the controversy surrounding George Washington's sterility, about how some biologists suspected he'd suffered from a condition called Klinefelter's aneuploidy—but I was too busy sketching out my own genetic tree to answer. For the thousandth time, I drew the adjacent ovals for my twin cousins, and a square with a diagonal line through it, for my Uncle Jesse, who'd committed suicide. These pedigrees were an exercise I performed to amuse myself, like tic-tac-toe or crossword puzzles. I always etched a dashed box alongside my own dark circle at the bottom of the chart, indicating my potential marriage to Jonah Driscoll.

"Abraham Lincoln," said Miss Stanley. "Many people believe President Lincoln suffered from a genetic disorder called Marfan's syndrome that makes people tall and thin, but also damages their hearts—"

The lunch bell cut her short. A dozen notebooks closed simultaneously.

"Don't go anywhere yet," ordered Miss Stanley, ensuring our collective animosity. "Please take out a piece of paper and write two or three sentences about your impressions of our first class. And pick up your homework. *Then* you can leave."

After only a few seconds of frantic tearing and scribbling, I was the final student remaining in the classroom. I wrote:

> *Dear Miss Stanley:*
> *On the whole, I think things are going well. But you did say we shouldn't be afraid to share ideas for improving class, so I just wanted you to know that many scientists no longer think*

Franklin Roosevelt had polio. More likely, he suffered from an atypical form of Guillain-Barré syndrome. Also, while some people do believe Abraham Lincoln had Marfan's disease, they are probably wrong. The vast majority of men and women with long legs are perfectly healthy—what you might call normal variants. I do hope you will share all of this with the rest of the class . . . because anyone is entitled to her own opinion, but not her own facts. Good luck with veterinary school!
Sincerely, Natalie Limberg (Louise on your attendance sheet)

I slid my note into the pile beside our teacher's sickly African violet. I wanted to search through the other comments, to see what Jonah had written, but Miss Stanley practically yanked the stack of torn loose-leaf from my hands.

. . . . .

That evening was my mother's therapy session, so my father took me to the Hogarth Mall to play Physical Diagnosis. It was a game we'd shared since my earliest childhood: during long road trips, and while waiting in line at the post office, and even on those rare holidays when my mother dragged dad and me to synagogue. It was also the *only* game my father ever played with me, the one occasion on which he allowed himself to be frivolous. The object of "PD"—as bizarre as I realize this will sound—was to identify genetic diseases in strangers. Some diagnoses were easy, like the elfin features of Williams syndrome or the truncated pinkies of Albright's osteodystrophy. But my father prided himself on being able to distinguish a child with an apparent toothache from inherited cherubism, and a harmless allergy from postprandial snatiation, a rare familial ailment in which the full stomach causes vigorous sneezing. As a young girl, I loved this game because it affirmed my father's genius. Genetic knowledge, in his hands, was virtually

X-ray vision. Later, as a teenager, I wielded this same wisdom as a weapon: No matter how unattractive I was—no matter how wide my hip bones grew—I could wander along Olney Boulevard and see a man's heart defect in his eyebrows.

The Hogarth Mall was only five years old. I remembered when the space had housed a horseback riding stable and a "pick-your-own-pumpkins" patch, then the long months when it was an irregular mud plain patrolled by Caterpillar backhoes. (The mall was part of the county's futile effort to revitalize an East Bay hard hit by the collapse of the domestic marine equipment industry; instead, its national chain stores rapidly drove most of Creve Coeur's Main Street out of business.) My father liked to stake out a circular table in the food court, opposite the glass elevator. He'd pour a two-ounce package of maple syrup into his coffee, a habit he'd picked up from Grandpa Saul, and he'd ask me about my school day while his eyes scanned the passing shoppers for physical imperfections. Sometimes, middle-aged women would return his gaze—letting their eyes linger a moment too long on his strong jaw and handsome, thoughtful features. Even as a teenager, I was never embarrassed by him. He was far too serious and dignified for that. I had a difficult time understanding why he put up with my mother, who embarrassed me constantly by using words like "menstruation" and "orgasm," and who regularly lost her temper in public. That night, my father pointed out a pair of achondroplastic dwarves, strolling arm-in-arm, and a janitor with a mild case of acromegaly. He jotted down these sighting in his notepad, and, without looking up, asked me, "So, ninth grader, what's the news from the front lines?"

"I told my teachers I want to be called Natalie from now on."

"You're fourteen years old," said my father. "I suppose you're entitled to choose any name you want."

That made me feel guilty. As though rejecting "Louise" was rejecting him. But I couldn't imagine Jonah Driscoll kissing a girl with an old lady's name.

"You can still call me Louise *at home*," I said.

"Thank you," said my father. "I think I will."

He folded shut the notepad and tucked it into the breast pocket of his jacket. Then he removed his eyeglasses and cleaned them with a paper napkin.

"I learned something important today," I said. "I learned that I'm smarter than Miss Stanley, my new biology teacher. The only reason she's the teacher and I'm the student is because she's older than I am."

"That's probably true," he agreed. "But she's *still* the teacher."

My father's tone suggested the weariness of experience—that he'd also known what it was like to have teachers of mediocre intellect. I was well-versed in the story of how he'd been suspended from M.I.T. as a sophomore for hacking into the dean's private telephone line—and how he'd sent that same dean a newspaper clipping when he was named to the President's Council on Science and Technology.

"Oh, I almost forgot. I have homework for you," I announced.

"*For me*?"

"I need to find out ABO blood types. Yours. Mom's. All of my grandparents." I rummaged through my knapsack and retrieved the assignment.

I already knew that my father was a type-A. My mother was an O. That meant I'd have to be either one or the other. But Grandpa Saul was my sole surviving grandparent, and he lived in Boston with his crazy sister, Aunt Gertie, so I'd never had an opportunity to trace back any further.

My father skimmed over Miss Stanley's questions, and frowned. "So much for maintaining a semblance of genetic privacy," he said.

"In any case, I'm relatively confident that Grandma and Uncle Jesse were both type-B's, but I can ask Grandpa Saul on Sunday, to be sure." My father handed me back the assignment. "You'll have to talk to your mother about her parents. That may be harder to find out."

.....

The next morning, Miss Stanley phoned in sick, and an elderly substitute with sparse mauve hair showed us a film titled "The Secrets of Chromosomes." In the grainy footage, a class of about twenty white kids and one black girl take turns asking imbecilic questions: *Why do I have my father's chin?* and *My friend's sister has Down syndrome. Can I catch it?* Then crude graphics of double helices and karyotypes flashed on the screen, while the narrator—who looked like Mister Rogers and sounded like Gregory Peck in "To Kill A Mockingbird"—unlocked the so-called "mysteries" of molecular science. In the rear of *our* classroom, beside the plastic skeleton, Becky Timms and Zach Dorsey conducted a biology lesson of their own, using their tongues. Two seats away from me, Jonah Driscoll shaded an unflattering portrait of the substitute teacher in his sketchbook. I watched out of the corner of my eye as his large, mitt-like hands virtually loped back-and-forth across the page, capturing the old woman's dull, depleted eyes and tight-set mouth. In my imagination, I catch Jonah sketching *me* one afternoon, and I convince him of his great artistic potential. Eventually, he applies himself to his academic work and—with me as his model—he is admitted on a full scholarship to the Rhode Island School of Design. Of course, these were all fantasies. Jonah hadn't said two words to me since he'd joined our class in eighth grade, when his father took a job as the district's transportation and maintenance coordinator. When he looked up from his sketch of the old woman, I turned my head away quickly. At the end of the film, Shorty Foust asked the substitute whether the black girl was Mrs. Tubbs' daughter.

Miss Stanley returned the following day, looking far too refreshed for a woman who claimed "an early bout of the flu." She wore a maroon leather skirt and matching, high-heeled boots, revealing two-inches of bare calf. On the chalkboard, she wrote: *I. Discussion of ABO Blood Types. II. ABO Blood Type Laboratory*. Then she passed down each aisle—now more like a drill sergeant than a talk-show host—demanding to inspect our take-home assignments. I displayed mine, with question marks beside the blanks for my mother's parents. "They're dead," I explained—not mentioning that I'd forgotten to show my mom the form. Miss Stanley nodded indifferently and moved along. She shrugged when Lori Beckwith revealed that she was adopted, but she had done the homework anyway. She sniffed when the Zorinsky twins, Mia and Tia, handed in only one sheet between them. But Miss Stanley stopped cold when Jonah displayed an empty page. "Science is a collaborative effort," she declared. "You'll have to meet me halfway, if you intend to learn anything *at all* this semester. I'm truly disappointed."

Jonah tugged at the cuff of his denim jacket, his gaze focused on his desktop. I could easily have let the moment pass. Instead, I blurted out, "Maybe his parents don't know what their blood types are. You didn't even give him a chance to tell you."

Miss Stanley ignored me. She stood alongside Jonah's desk, frowning, tapping her fingertips together. If I'd expected Jonah to be appreciative of my intercession, I was wretchedly mistaken. He turned to look at me—as though he'd never seen me before—and he threw me a glare as toxic as a venomous dart. I felt the scalding poison traveling up my arteries into my forehead.

"Did you even *try* to do the assignment?" Miss Stanley asked him.

Jonah said nothing. My legs trembled under my desk.

Miss Stanley shook her head twice, for emphasis, and stepped briskly to the front of the room, as though inspecting the final row of students' homework wasn't worth her bother. "What exactly *is* a blood type?" she demanded of the class. Meanwhile, I tried to make eye contact with Jonah—to apologize with my face—but he'd returned to sketching, this time a vicious likeness of Miss Stanley.

Becky Timms raised her hand. "My mother read this diet book that, like, says people with different blood types should eat different foods."

Miss Stanley scanned the class, refusing to acknowledge this effort.

"Blood types determine who you can give blood to," said Lori Beckwith. "I have type O blood, which means I can give blood to anybody."

"What else?"

None of my classmates had anything more to say, so the silence dragged on. From the open window came the shouts of workmen constructing the new gymnasium, and the scent of freshly-sawed wood. I didn't want to speak, but I also didn't want Miss Stanley to think she knew more than me. "Blood groups are determined by the presence of antigens on red blood cells," I said. "Antibodies to antigens A and B can lead to transfusion incompatibility."

"Very good," said Miss Stanley. "Did you hear that, Jonah? You could learn a lot from Louise."

"Natalie," I corrected her. She didn't hear me, or chose not to.

"We have only forty-five minutes left," said Miss Stanley, picking up her designer handbag. "Please make efficient use of your time in the laboratory."

We crossed the corridor into the lab room, which we shared with the tenth grade chemistry classes. The equipment for that morning's exercise was already laid out like dinner utensils on the phenolic countertops, except for the diagnostic blood preparations, which were stored under the steel-coated fume hoods. Each work station had its own sterile lancet, stirring sticks and alcohol prep pads. All we had to do was prick our thumbs and mix our blood with the labeled samples. If we had type A blood, we'd form clumps with the B sample. If we had type B blood, we'd form clumps with the A sample. If we had type O blood, we'd form clumps with neither the A nor the B. It was all so simple, a well-trained chimp could have completed the experiment—except that she'd have the wrong blood proteins. Miss Stanley distributed a worksheet with problems to be filled out at the conclusion of the session.

"Any questions?" she asked.

"I've got one," said Shorty Foust. "We never finished our introductions."

Miss Stanley appeared surprised—she'd clearly forgotten her omission—but luckily for her, the rest of us had already started dispersing around the laboratory. I examined my reflection in the industrial sink, combing my hair forward to make my forehead look shorter. Then I dug my fingernails deep into my palms and walked straight up to Jonah, who was grinning while his friends played a shell game with three paper cups and a quarter. If he saw me approaching, he pretended that he didn't.

"Look, I'm sorry," I said. "That was a really stupid thing for me to say."

Jonah unwrapped a toothpick and let it droop at the corner of his mouth.

"Not a big deal," he answered—sounding genuinely sheepish. "Say, Louise. You're the genius. How do we do this thing?"

Natalie, I wanted to shout. *Natalie!*

I could have strangled Miss Stanley for her earlier mistake.

"Yeah, Louise," said one of Jonah's friends. "You've got to help us."

So I sat down between Jonah and Sean Fuccillo, with Zach Dorsey and half a dozen other popular boys crowded behind me. I could feel the heat of their bodies, their collective bulk hemming me in.

"It's really easy," I said. "The only hard part is sticking yourself."

I demonstrated by pricking my finger and mixing the blood into the preparation with the group-B antibodies. To my surprise, the combination formed a thick, gelatinous clump. "The sample must be contaminated," I explained. "Let me try a different container." So I retrieved the ketchup-style bottle from a second fume hood and repeated the experiment, but the results came out identically. Every time I pooled my blood with the diagnostic preparation, the combined product insisted that my veins contained type-B blood. In the general population, this wasn't a rare finding—and certainly not a cause for medical concern. It was merely a biological impossibility in the daughter of a type-A father and a type-O mother. Eventually, I gave up trying, and I told Miss Stanley I was feeling nauseous. She gave me permission to visit the school nurse's office, but instead I climbed up the hill behind the high school and, my head spinning, ran down Meriwether Street until the Gothic dormers of Commodore Perry were no longer visible behind the heads of the molting beech trees.

.....

I didn't want to return to school and I didn't want to go home, so I roamed downtown Creve Coeur until the whitewashed cape codders along Harpoon Street glowed orange and pink under the sinking sun. I realized my options were few: The courageous choice would have been to confront my parents with the damning clumps of blood and demand to know whether I had been adopted—or worse. As my imagination lurched into overdrive, I dreamed up far-fetched scenarios in which I'd been wrested from leftist dissidents during the Argentine Dirty War or purchased on the black market from Romanian Gypsies. Of course, neither of these accounts explained how I'd come to be saddled with my mother's narrowly-set eyes and Grandpa Saul's colossal masculine brow. So my other alternative was to block out the entire incident—to chalk it up to a genetic fluke, some sort of one-in-a-billion mutation—and to continue life as my parents' biological daughter. In the movies, I would have had a confidante to help with this decision, a devoted step-sister, or a benevolent aunt, or a pair of equally unpopular friends, maybe twins, but the reality was that I didn't have anyone to share my burden. Big-boned, broad-framed girls with oversized foreheads usually don't—no matter how smart they are—not, at least, until college.

At first, I wandered aimlessly. Eventually, I tramped across the Farragut Avenue Bridge and followed the elevated gravel bed of the abandoned streetcar line out to the Irish Flats. This was a well-tended, working-class community—rough by Creve Coeur's standards, but not particularly dangerous—where Portuguese and Cape Verdean immigrants had long since supplanted the last sons and daughters of Erin. Only in the names of a smattering of mom-and-pop businesses did the neighborhood still cling to its roots: Londonderry Lanes, Kavanagh's Spa & Soda Fountain, a formalwear shop called Donnelly & Regan. Sullivan's Saloon, where Jonah's mother served drinks, was a freestanding roadhouse opposite a lumber yard. Behind the building lay a pond where young children came to feed ducks and—after dark—boys like Jonah Driscoll and his friends consumed alcohol with relative impunity. I ambled around to the far side of the stagnant water, taking stock of the crushed beer cans. Sometimes, even on weekdays, Jonah's friends would gather here to drink. I knew this because, on several occasions that summer, I'd trekked all the way out to the Irish flats myself—nearly three miles from my own house—hoping that, if I placed my body in closer proximity to Jonah's, a miracle might attend to the rest. But it didn't. And I'd never had the courage to advance any closer than the shoulder of the county highway—near enough to hear him laughing, but not for him to see me. Now, I settled onto a freshly-hewn tree stump and lopped the heads off the surrounding toadstools with a stick. As twilight descended, I carved out an almost perfect circle of decapitated fungi. Jays and wide-winged flickers thrashed in the intense brush overhead. A damp chill ran down my spine, and I shivered. I hoped Jonah might discover me here—that he might rescue me that night, as I'd often planned to rescue him—but it was still far too early in the evening.

I can't say how long I'd been waiting at the pond—or even if I'd genuinely been waiting for him at all—when the inspiration first came to me. It was an insane idea, the sort of cockeyed plot that desperate women hatched up on daytime soap operas, but that didn't mean it couldn't work. After all, Jonah was a decent guy. Moreover, I'd seen his father at Commodore Perry, supervising the busses—a cheerful, burly man with pale jowls and a walrus mustache—and I sensed Anthony Driscoll would expect his son to do "the right thing" under the circumstances. So here was my opportunity: If I could only find a way for Jonah to get me pregnant, maybe while in an alcoholic haze, I told myself that I'd have a good chance of keeping him forever. That would be the best *for both of us*. Because once he'd spent enough time with me, and realized how much I loved him, he would forget that I wore a size-14 dress and extra-wide sneakers. In a matter of minutes, I had our futures planned out: Jonah would create his art at home while he tended to the baby, freelancing *New Yorker* covers on the side to pay our bills, and I'd go to graduate school at Harvard in computational genomics. I was scared about becoming pregnant, of course. I was only fourteen. Who wouldn't be nervous in my shoes? But the more I reflected upon my new scheme, the more convinced I became that it might prove the antidote to all of my suffering.

I hiked home at a brisk clip, buoyed by romantic hope. I was as giddy as the merriest drinker on the dance floor at the roadhouse. A nippy fog had blown in off the harbor, swathing the hollows at the foot of Banker's Hill, leaving its clammy print on the dead leaves heaped at the curbside. It was well past suppertime. I expected that my parents might be alarmed, or even angry at me, but I wasn't concerned. For the duration of that brief three mile walk, I didn't care about whether I'd been baby-knapped, or purchased from a peddler's cart, or concocted in a test tube as part of a high school science experiment. I believed that even an unattractive changeling with type-B blood, if she played her cards right, had a chance to be loved. But as home drew nearer, my optimism faded. Something about the familiar lights of our dreary ranch house—soggy chrysanthemums lining the slate walkway, the iron rooster perched atop the weather vane—reminded me that I wasn't the type of girl who got herself pregnant at fourteen. There were gutsy, free-spirited girls who would willingly take that kind of risk to win the heart of a boy like Jonah Driscoll. But those girls didn't need to.

.....

I arrived home to find my parents arguing bitterly. This was a ritual they'd gone through at least once each month since my earliest memories—a domestic Jewish variation on kabuki theatre. My father sat silently at the kitchen table, looking like an old-time newspaper editor with his tie hanging loose around his thick neck and his shirtsleeves bunched up at the elbows. It was impossible to tell whether his grim expression reflected displeasure, or merely indifference. Meanwhile, my mother paced the linoleum in her threadbare orange bathrobe. She rubbed her hands anxiously—like Lady Macbeth in the senior class play—and called my father a "shit-fucker" and a "selfish bastard" who couldn't be trusted. She accused him of ruining her life, of using up her "good years" and spitting her out once she'd passed forty. The offense, in this instance, was that my father had agreed to deliver a lecture in Denver, Colorado the following Saturday, without first consulting her. Neither of them seemed to care that I'd come home so late. I raided the refrigerator and leaned against the granite countertop in the cooking island, gorging myself on cold pizza.

"I'm sorry there's no dinner, Louise," said my mother. "Your asshole of a father got me too upset to cook anything."

"It's okay," I said. "But please stop shouting."

"Nobody's shouting," shouted my mother. She balled her fists together and sucked her breath through her clenched teeth—producing the distinctive feral slurp that she often made when she grew too enraged for words. It was difficult to imagine that this same frenzied woman had once played the harp professionally, lulling admiring audiences into mellifluous bliss, before she'd given up music to stay home with me. "Shit. Fuck. Shit," she screamed. "I can't help it if your father views his family as an impediment to his goddam Nobel Prize."

"Please watch your language," said my father.

My mother responded with an ugly grimace. "That's five weekends in a row, Gordon.... What's the point?"

"You could come with me," answered my father. "They'll pay for your ticket."

"Great. So I can spend all day in hotel bar with a pack of dried-up hens while you and your genome buddies bore each other to tears. That's some offer."

My mother's voice had softened slightly. I knew this was the point where they'd inch their way toward a truce—that, as incomprehensible as it seemed to me, this would be one of the nights when they'd close the bedroom door behind them. I poured myself a tall mug of Diet Coke and let the fizz settle. "I want to say something," I said.

They both looked up. They seemed surprised that I was still in the room.

"What's wrong, honey," said my mother. "You aren't getting sick, are you?"

She crossed the kitchen and felt my brow with the back of her chilly hand. I pulled my head away. "She feels warm to me, Gordon," said my mother.

"I have type-B blood," I announced.

My mother tried to feel my brow again, but I wouldn't let her. "I think she's coming down with something."

"You're not listening to me," I said. Louder. "We did an experiment in Miss Stanley's class and my blood clumped when it was exposed to type-B antibodies. That means I can't be the biological child of a type-A father and a type-O mother."

My mother still didn't appear interested. She started asking me a litany of inane questions: *Did my throat hurt? Had I been out in the rain?* But now my father's penetrating eyes were trained on me like a rifle, aglow with the same intensity that he employed to scan strangers for genetic deformities. He rose from the table and approached so quickly, for a moment I feared he might shake me.

"You're *sure* it was type-B?" he asked.

"I tried six times," I answered.

"The antibodies were probably contaminated," said my father. "I'll bet this sort of mistake happens all the time."

"They weren't contaminated. Everybody else's results came out right."

"They *must* have been contaminated," he answered. "Now go to you room."

My mother had stopped asking about my symptoms. She bit her knuckles between her lips as she realized that something was deeply amiss.

"I said go to your room, Louise," warned my father—his tone sharper than I could ever remember it. "I want to speak to your mother *in private*. Go to your room this minute and close your door."

I looked to my mother, but her expression was equally glacial, so I scooped two more slices of pizza from the box and retreated up the stairs.

.....

I sat in bed, staring at the ceiling. The furnishings in my bedroom hadn't changed significantly since my parents had purchased the house, shortly after my fourth birthday. A mobile of fluorescent fish still dangled from the exposed rafters, above the space that had once housed my playpen. Over the years, grade by grade, I'd acquired personal junk—but I hadn't shed any—so my chess & checkers board and my college genetics textbooks sat beside my tinker toys and Legos inside the pink wooden cabinet that my mother had once hand-painted with giant butterflies. It was a small, cheerless garret of a room and I spent as little time there as possible, but I'd cried myself to sleep on that bed far too frequently: when Grandma Pauline died, after nobody invited me to the junior high school prom, the numerous times I'd seen Jonah Driscoll hanging out with Becky Timms. Or Samantha Malinek, or any of the countless petite creatures who might, or might not, have been his girlfriends. I wasn't stupid, of course. Rationally, I realized there was nothing so extraordinarily special about Jonah, except that at some point I'd decided to love him *and only him*. I'd made a conscious choice—and now it was impossible to imagine starting over again, to concede defeat and fall in love with somebody else. Sometimes, I suspected that my father felt that way about my mother. That he'd invested too much in her to quit. I wiped my tears on my stuffed, earless panda and edged open the bedroom door. Then I tiptoed along the foyer carpet, perching myself between the linen closet and the stairs.

My parents' second argument of the evening was approaching a crescendo.

"We're talking in circles, Gordon," said my mother. "I can't take any more of this blood type bullshit. It's just like you told her—*it's a mistake*.... Take a look in a goddam mirror. She looks just like you."

A long pause followed. All I could hear were the steady murmur of the refrigerator and the tinny sighs of the plumbing. I inched myself down onto the top step.

"So you want me to actually say it," my father finally answered—his voice icy, matter-of-fact, as though debating a scientific theory.

"Say *what*?"

"You know what, Jeanne. You know *exactly* who the girl looks like."

My mother's slippers shuffled across the flooring. "I thought we'd put this all behind us," she said. "Jesus Christ, Gordon. That was *fourteen* years ago."

"Precisely," snapped my father. "Fourteen years ago. *You* said it. Not me."

Glass shattered in reply. My mother had thrown a coffee cup against the exposed brickwork of the kitchen, and porcelain shards ricocheted into the front hall. "I won't play this game, Gordon," she threatened. "Fourteen years ago was the time to talk about blood types. You have no right—You can't choose to be willfully blind and—"

"I shouldn't have to be willfully blind!"

"You don't *have* to be anything," shouted my mother. I could hear the sobs shuddering in her throat. "He's dead, Goddamit. Hasn't everyone suffered enough?"

It wasn't until that moment that I realized they'd been arguing about Uncle Jesse. My father's younger brother had been a mathematics prodigy, and a talented bass player, but he'd never lived up to any of his potential. Princeton dismissed him for lackluster attendance, and he squandered most of the Reagan years drifting from garage band to garage band—and from girlfriend's apartment to fleabag motel. By the time he'd overdosed on antifreeze at the age of twenty-nine, he'd been crashing on the sofa in my parents' living room for nearly a year. That was the same November the Berlin Wall fell, six months before I was born. Nobody in the family spoke much about Jesse Limberg anymore, and we didn't have photos of him atop the piano. All I really knew about the man was that he'd had type-B blood, and a pronounced widow's peak, and a serious case of food allergies as a grade-schooler. Now I'd learned one thing more.

"Please, Gordon," said my mother—calmer, drained. "It's not my fault she did that experiment. I can't take this anymore."

"I wish she hadn't done it either. That's not the point."

"What *is* the point?" my mother demanded. "What do you want me to do?"

"I'll tell you what we're going to do," replied my father. He lowered his voice and I had to strain to hear him. "We're going to have a talk with that idiot teacher of hers, and we're going to make it clear to Louise that this has all been a terrible misunderstanding. You'll know that's not true. And I'll know that's not true. But Louise won't—and you are not going to tell her otherwise. *Not ever.* Do you understand me?"

"Don't talk to me in that tone," said my mother. "I'm not a child."

I snuck away only seconds before she stormed upstairs, slamming the bedroom door so hard that she rattled the entire house.

.....

We drove out to Commodore Perry as a family the following Monday. This was the first late afternoon appointment that Miss Stanley claimed to have available. In the interim, my parents spoke to me as though nothing were out of the ordinary, but with a peculiar wariness, as though they had been replaced by body snatchers. They rarely addressed each other at all. One night, my father didn't return home until three o'clock in the morning. He awakened my mother by rapping his knuckles against their bedroom door, demanded a pillow from the master bed, and retreated to the foldaway cot in the downstairs guest room. The next evening, my mother went to her therapy session, but my father didn't take me to the mall for our usual game of Physical Diagnosis. I had no need to ask why. Even the thought of sketching a family history or diagnosing a stranger made my throat muscles tighten. So when the day finally arrived for our group meeting with Miss Stanley, I would have done anything to have never mentioned the blood-type experiment to my parents. I offered a deal to God—a God I was not at all certain I believed in: If He allowed my family life return to normal, or as close to normal as it had been previously, I wouldn't ask Him for any more help with Jonah Driscoll. But even as I made this promise, I realized that I would never be able to keep it. I was already self-aware enough to recognize my own limitations.

It was a crisp, clear day—chilly for late September. I rode the bus home from school and draped myself across a chaise-longue on the patio, listening to the soundtrack from *Grease*, while I waited for my father to return from teaching. My mother watched a game show on the black-and-white television in the kitchen. She painted her nails—fuchsia—and then aired them dry. She'd had her hair done that morning, a flared bob. I don't know whether she was trying to look her best for my father's sake, or Miss Stanley's—or possibly she just wanted to please herself. For my own part, I kept on the same torn dungarees and baggy "Geology Rocks" sweatshirt that I'd worn all day. Yet, when we finally crammed into my father's hybrid Toyota coup, none of us speaking, I felt as confined in my casual clothes as I usually did when I wore a wool skirt and pantyhose to synagogue on Yom Kippur. Never had the ten minute drive through downtown Creve Coeur seemed so endless, so exhausting.

The visitor's parking lot at Commodore Perry stood nearly empty. Out on the playing fields, the junior varsity football team was locked in a scrimmage—blue-on-gold uniforms sacking each other in internecine pantomime. Zach Dorsey was out there. And Sean Fuccillo. But not Jonah. My crush was a working-class guy—and ruggedly handsome—so he didn't need to prove himself by pummeling his friends. I was grateful for that, because it meant he wasn't on campus that late. I was afraid that if we ran into him, my father might feel entitled to explain the purpose of our family's visit. As friendless as I already was, that would have been social suicide. The wounds were still fresh from an incident the previous winter, when the diplomat father of a Yemeni boy named Hassoun had argued with Mrs. Satnick about the appropriate role for evolution in the eighth grade science curriculum. The son had actually been a really decent guy—not popular, but bright and friendly. But after Mrs. Satnick recounted the episode indignantly for her honors students, my classmates started calling the boy "Six Days," for the length of time required to create the universe. Eventually, he changed schools. I'd already tried to convince my father to cancel our own meeting, but he answered, "I can accept poor teaching, but I cannot tolerate bad science." And that was that.

We pulled into a parking space along the flooded drainage canal, adjacent to the asphalt patch marked PRINCIPAL. My mother folded her arms across her chest. "I've changed my mind, Gordon," she said. "I'll wait in the car."

"We're *all* going inside," answered my father. "We're going as a family."

They exchanged looks of mutual hostility. I feared they might sit like this for hours, each holding out for the other to yield, like in that children's book, where the two stubborn hunters fight over a glass of cold water during a snowstorm. But suddenly my mother snapped, "Fine," and thrust open her car door. I waited for her to pop the seat forward—grateful when I could finally stretch my legs. My father asked me where the biology classroom was located, then led the way down the darkened passage.

Miss Stanley was reading an airport novel when we entered, a water-stained volume with a lipstick kiss embossed on the glossy cover. She folded the book open to hold her place and set it down beside *Veterinary School Made Simple*. "Dr. Limberg," she said, extending her small, stiff hand. "Mrs. Limberg."

My teacher was sporting a low-cut blouse that revealed far too much cleavage, and a pair of large earrings shaped like elephants. I tried to picture her as a man might—*as my father might*—and I focused on her imperial nose and jutting chin. No quantity of makeup or jewelry could mask these damning features. Yet what amazed me most about this pathetic woman was that she clearly saw none of this. Miss Stanley genuinely believed that she was pretty. "Please sit down," she said. "But as I told you on the phone, Dr. Limberg, I'm not exactly sure how I can help you." She glanced at me nervously, biting her lip. "Honestly, I didn't expect you to bring Louise along."

"*Natalie,*" I said fiercely.

"Not now, Louise," said my mother. "*Please.*"

"Maybe Louise would like to wait outside," suggested Miss Stanley.

"I want my daughter to hear this. It's important," replied my father. "I don't believe in keeping secrets."

"I just thought..." said Miss Stanley, but she let her sentence trail off.

I hopped onto the top of a front-row desk and let my feet dangle off the edge. My mother remained standing by the open door, clutching her handbag to her chest.

"Let me cut to the chase, Miss Stanley," said my father. "Louise tells me that you conducted a so-called blood typing laboratory without explaining to the students that ABO blood types aren't inherited in a strictly Mendelian manner. To put it bluntly, you've scared my daughter into questioning her paternity."

"As I told you on the phone—"

"What you've done is thoroughly irresponsible," interjected my father, his voice rising. "You do understand that, don't you? You owed it to these children to inform them that sometimes—often—the results of agglutination tests can be highly misleading." My father leaned forward, his finger inches from Miss Stanley's eyes. "The *least* you can do to right the matter is to set the record straight."

"Please, Gordon," pleaded my mother.

"Blood type means nothing. *Nothing,*" continued my father. His face was suffusing a reddish-grey, his neck veins bulging. "You're a professional, aren't you? Of all people, you ought to recognize that." I'd never heard one adult dress down another like that—and I feared Miss Stanley might summon the principal. Or the police. But she appeared far too shocked to assess her options.

"I'm not sure what to say, really," stammered Miss Stanley. "I'd like to help you, Dr. Limberg, but you know as well as I do that science is science. I mean: You can't choose your own genetics."

That must have been the opening my father had wanted. He removed a manila folder from the breast pocket of his jacket and slapped it down on Miss Stanley's desk. "What do you know about Bombay genes?" he demanded. "What have you read about Shoenhoff-Ballinger variants? Here are forty-two case reports of type-A parents producing type-B offspring. *Forty-two*. And that's only right here in Rhode Island." As my father spoke, he fanned the contents of the folder across Miss Stanley's desk. "In the future, I suggest you do your homework. I've spent twenty-two years studying these things, and quite frankly, *you're the one* trying to choose your own genetics."

Miss Stanley surveyed the papers helplessly. "Bombay genes," she echoed. She clutched the back of her desk chair, her knuckles turning white. "Look, I'm really . . . I'm just really . . ." But whatever Miss Stanley really was, she never told us.

"I trust you'll set the record straight, Miss Stanley," said my father.

He did not wait for an answer. He looked at my mother—then at me—then back at my mother—and he strode quickly out of the classroom.

We followed him silently through the empty, dimly-lit corridors into the gray parking lot. I'd never before seen my father lose his temper—*not like that*. I was far too stunned to speak. When we arrived at the car, my mother said, "Sometimes I think my entire life has been one large mistake after another." She spoke to nobody in particular, maybe to the wind, as though she were sharing the final moments of an argument she'd been having with herself.

.....

I waited another two hours in my childhood bedroom. I could hear my father and mother negotiating in the kitchen—their voices sounding gentler, almost reasonable, though I couldn't make out the individual words. It didn't matter. I'd crossed that threshold where I would never again eavesdrop on my parents' conversations, because I no longer desired to be privy to their secrets. When they finally climbed the stairs, long after ten o'clock, my father was telling a story about his own eighth grade teacher and how she'd caught the hem of her ankle-length dress in an incubator hatch. This no longer surprised me: I suppose it was part of the compromise, the ongoing settlement, that made their lives bearable. They both poked their heads into my room, to tell me that they loved me—without any acknowledgement of the afternoon's humiliating debacle. My mother, for once, was smiling. Then they continued down the hall and shut their own bedroom door. If I'd listened closely, I'd have been able to hear them for hours. Instead, I tiptoed down to the entryway and retrieved my down jacket from the front closet.

The wind had picked up after sundown and the angry gusts rattled the metal street signs. I pulled the hood of my sweatshirt tight around my ears and hiked across the Farragut Avenue Bridge, traveling as quickly as my lungs would allow. Out on the county highway, the street lamps hadn't been lit. I had to duck into the bushes repeatedly to avoid oncoming headlights. Briars clung to the legs of my dungarees, and prickled the tops of my socks, but I gave up trying to pluck them off. Several times, I stepped into frigid puddles, and my toes began to burn. Only when I reached the pullout for Sullivan's saloon did it I consider the possibility that Jonah Driscoll was at home in bed.

Country music pulsed from the open door of the roadhouse, where the bouncer rested eyes-closed under the blinking blue-neon signs. I followed the edge of the gravel parking lot until I reached the footpath that circled the pond. I could hear loud, easy conversation, and reggae music playing on a radio. Flashlight beams cut wildly across the dense grove of evergreens. I paused about twenty yards below the partiers, listening for Jonah's crisp, laconic voice. All I could make out were cheers, and waves of impenetrable chatter—and then silence. But the last sound I heard, before the woods turned mute, was Jonah asking an unseen companion to pass him another beer.

"Quick. Someone's coming!" cried one boy.

"Are you sure?" demanded another.

All of the voices were male. Some were unfamiliar.

"It's only me," I called to them. "It's Natalie. Natalie Limberg!"

I heard one boy ask something indecipherable, and then Jonah's answer, "You know, Natalie. *Louise*." His words were thick and slurred, as though blood were pooling around his tongue. "Louise *Natalie*," he repeated. "Natalie *Louise*." And then his speech shattered into a fit of deep, resonant laughter. I followed those laughs up the hillside, through the thorns and the darkness, his drunken amusement beckoning me toward the first of my life-altering mistakes.

Creve Coeur

The woman who was not my mother was named Sheila Stanton and at the age of nineteen she was held captive for ninety-one days by the Red Ribbon Strangler. That was during 1967, the Summer of Love. After she was freed by a SWAT team, Stanton found herself the nation's celebrity *du jour*. She performed a duet of "Rescue Me" with Aretha Franklin on the Ed Sullivan Show and went on to win a pair of back-to-back Grammy nominations for her folk-rock ballads "Don't Hold Me Hostage" and "Stockholm Syndrome." Growing up in Creve Coeur, Rhode Island—whose other claim on history was a late-life visit by Lizzie Borden—my male classmates all passed through a phase where they begged their parents to let them trick-or-treat disguised as the kidnapper.

By the time I was conscious enough to be interested—at the height of the first Reagan recession—the Red Ribbon Strangler, Wayne Zane Minsky, was long dead. Natural causes: an antibiotic-resistant skin infection. The serial killer had been five months into a three-hundred-plus year sentence, and he'd never explained what motivated him to spare his final victim—why he hadn't abandoned Stanton's naked body on a front lawn or porch swing with a crimson bow festooning her waist. But what interested us most in grade school wasn't the psychology, it was the house. Every weekday, my bus climbed Banker's Hill, past the three story Victorian mansion from whose flagstone path Stanton had been abducted. Towering hollyhocks dominated the steep street-front garden, punctuated by stands of sinewy tiger lilies. An American flag hung backwards on the door-face; the brass knocker was an owl wearing spectacles. One Thanksgiving, the LaRue brothers and I made a closer investigation of the crime scene, which had been constructed, according to the plaque on the portico, by a retired whaling magnate. We were examining the walkway for bloodstains when a plump, small-eyed matron came to the door and asked courteously what we wanted in her hedges. We ran off. For many years afterward, I mistakenly believed this to be Sheila Stanton's mother.

As for my father: If he ever wondered about his ex-fiancée, he didn't let on. His concerns were those of an ambitious but thoroughly small-time lighting retailer: Christmas displays in December, fireworks shows in July, staving off discount merchandisers during the slow months in between. Also getting me a university education, transforming his only son into a diplomat or a law professor—in short, anything far removed from the grind of Spring Clearance Sales and voltage conversion. So when my parents argued, it was over whether it was safe for me to go target shooting with Eddie LaRue and his uncle. Or how much they could afford to spend on a sailboat. Or if Gary Hart's affair with Donna Rice made him, in my father's words, "un-Presidential." But *never* about old flames or new temptations. Those possibilities were miles off either of their radar screens. On the rare occasions that a Sheila Stanton ballad played over the car radio, my mother didn't even care enough to switch the station.

.....

One August—the summer I turned fifteen—my father decided to expand and remodel his showroom. He quadrupled the floor space to nearly sixty thousand feet, buying out the blind Judaica dealer and the two Portuguese bait vendors who had hemmed in the enterprise since Grandpa Abe founded it in 1958. The highlight of the renovation was a store-length panorama of the Providence, Rhode Island, skyline, looking north from Narragansett Bay—every office window illuminated with a twinkle bulb. Another section of wall, beyond the alcove for ceiling fans, had been fashioned into the façade of a Tudor-style house. Hurricane lamps dangled from the porch beams; starlight stakes lined the "walkway"; topiary grizzly bears frolicked in the "yard." Dad even invested in a SnoBlaster for generating paper blizzards—bought at auction from a local company that had recently filmed a mouthwash commercial—to bestow on the sham dwelling-front a convincing pre-Christmas air. But true to his nature, my father built all of this on the location of the old shop, at the base of Banker's Hill, while the rest of the Creve Coeur business establishment was shifting piecemeal toward the commercial strips opposite the Washington County mall and along Route One. So only a handful of customers were on hand for the debut of the snow machine.

The contraption's maiden-run took place at mid-morning. Dad spoke from the Victorian "porch" like a political candidate addressing a rally, promising the sales staff a summer of ice storms and igloos. He wore the same uniform as the most junior clerk: a gray sports jacket, red suspenders and a tie depicting Thomas Edison holding up his first light bulb. All that set my father apart was his bushy salt-and-pepper mustache. The store's employees—and that included me, in my first summer job—were required to be clean-shaven. A legacy of Grandpa Abe. Next to Dad on the podium stood Carl Pachinsky, his chief electrician, fussing with the dials of the SnoBlaster. Pachinsky was a pear-shaped man who wore dark-blue coveralls like a second skin and who'd reached the age where he serenaded himself while working. *Un*self-consciously. During breaks in my father's oration, we heard snippets of *Sweet Caroline* and *Leaving on a Jet Plane*. Then, without much buildup, Dad ordered Pachinsky to yank the starter, and "the skies" opened. The sales staff clapped tepidly and returned to their posts. At that moment, the girl—the most alluring creature I've ever seen—stepped angelically into our artificial winter. She wore a low-cut white sundress and tiny white sneakers.

"I'm looking for Mr. Dortmund," she said. Her voice held just a hint of drama, a dash of New England royalty, as though she'd learned English watching Rosalind Russell movies. She also had a desperate force about her, like a talented actress holding together a very bad play. "Ma*ma* sent me to find Mr. Dortmund."

"Did she now?" asked my father.

Carl Pachinsky slapped my father on the back and said, "Fifteen will get you twenty, pal," far too loud, before shuffling off. I longed to choke the bloated ape from behind with electrical cord. The girl blushed. My father stretched his shoulders, squeezing the blades together like turkey wings; folds of skin rippled like lava waves at the base of his scalp.

"Ma*ma* wants you to help her put in a chandelier," said the girl.

"I see," said Dad. I sensed he was offended, but he held it in. "Well, what your mother needs is an electrician. Lots of those in the Yellow Pages. But this is a lighting distributorship. A *store*. We *install* only what we *sell*." He spoke so politely, so intimately, I feared he might wrap his arm around the girl's shoulders. He didn't. "You tell your mother, look in the telephone book."

"Ma*ma* said you might not want to come," said the girl. Her expression was graciously indifferent, almost indulgent. "She said to tell you it was *Sheila Stanton* who wanted you, and you'd find a few minutes."

"Oh, Jesus," said my father. At first, he didn't show much emotion—his look was almost one of mild displeasure—and flakes of paper snow began to build up on his hair. But then he grinned as though this were a punch-line to a joke told many years before. "So you're Sheila's daughter," he said.

"Step-daughter, strictly-speaking. Pamella. With two L's."

"Step-daughter," agreed my father. "Of course."

"But my father is dead," Pamella said, matter-of-fact. "He burned himself freebasing. My birthmother belongs to a religious order in Utah. They're like nuns, only not Catholic. She's *unfit*, so I don't see her." The girl sighed. She sounded more amused than pained. "I've been quite unlucky in that way."

"Well, Pamella with two L's," said my father. "I suppose I could spare of few minutes for an old friend." He retrieved his toolbox. "Hey, Wade," he said. "Introduce yourself to Pamella with two L's."

"Hi," I said. Then, after too long a pause, I added, "I'm Wade."

"I'm Pamella." She shook my hand crisply as though confirming a business transaction. She did not mention the two L's.

"She's pretty, Wade, isn't she?" asked my father. He had a knack for expressing sober what most men only dared say drunk. From a great distance came the shrill voice of a junior salesman pitching ceramic wall-sconces. "A very pretty girl," Dad repeated. "I bet you'll make someone a great girlfriend."

"Thank you," said Pamella.

"Your mother was a great girlfriend," he said. He was speaking about Pamella's mother, not mine. "You two could have been brother and sister, you know that?"

That was the sort of thing my father used to say often. Soft on logic, but as potentially lethal as a live current.

.....

We followed Pamella up the hill, over jagged sidewalks. Many of the once-fashionable homes had fallen into severe disrepair. Here and there, a tidy patch of marigolds or cherry tomatoes separated yards overgrown with crabgrass and pachysandra. College fraternities, exiled from the main campus, had unfurled their banners from several dormer windows. To my amazement, the girl led us directly to the crime scene. Inside, the house was dark and hot and smelled richly of aged wood. We crossed an unfurnished anterior room where cardboard boxes labeled "FRONT PARLOR" lay haphazardly around a pair of escritoires and a sofa, like boulders strewn about by a glacier. In the next room, Sheila Stanton was on her knees beside a long mahogany dining table. She'd been unwrapping crystal crockery, piece by piece, and stacking it on a rosewood sideboard. A chandelier socket gaped in the ceiling. When we arrived, Sheila, who was beak-nosed, with a chest as flat as an ironing board, rummaged through an oversized leather handbag and retrieved a pack of Virginia Slims. Mentholated. "I'm done with singing," she said, lighting a cigarette. "Now I can kill myself."

My father set his toolbox on the tabletop. Light from the high, curtain-less windows accentuated the ruts in his face. "Well, Sheila," he said. "I didn't know if I'd see you again."

"It's me," she said. "You're seeing me again."

My father's fingers toyed with the clasps on the toolbox, but he didn't take his eyes off her. I stood behind him. It struck me that despite her lack of cleavage, and a nose to rival Julius Caesar's, Sheila Stanton was somehow extremely alluring. "Yes," said my father. "I'm seeing you again."

She answered with a short, high-pitched laugh. "Do you like what you see?"

That shook Dad from his spell. "You're looking to put in a chandelier?"

"Oh, that," said Sheila. Seemingly annoyed. "In there."

My father had me remove the chandelier from a dust-coated garbage bag. The fixture was a four-armed hanging lamp with thirty-two small-watt bulbs. Not a model anyone had stocked in years. "This is my son, Wade," said my father. "He's going to be a diplomat or a law professor."

Sheila nodded at me. Totally indifferent. "I do appreciate this. I don't know what I'd have done without you." She tamped out the cigarette in a dainty porcelain candy dish. "I bet you're surprised I bought the house back."

"Somewhat," Dad agreed. "Do you know what the old chandelier looked like?"

Sheila shrugged. "Is that important? Why get hung up on the past?"

"The junction box has to be the right size," said my father.

"Does it?" Sheila sounded playful.

"It does," my father said firmly. "Otherwise, it'll come down on you and take half the ceiling with it. I'm going to have to put in a new box, just to be safe."

"Whatever. As long as you don't electrocute yourself." Sheila lit a second cigarette off the first, and addressed Pamella: "Why don't you give Wade a tour? Show him the roof. Charlie and I have catching up to do."

I looked to my dad. I was on the job, after all. "Go ahead," he said.

So, with overwhelming ambivalence, I followed Pamella through the partially furnished living room, and up a narrow wooden staircase, onto the open-air catwalk that connected two rear balconies. Outside, the breeze rustled the branches of the hundred-year-old oaks. Through a break in the leaves, you could see all of Creve Coeur: the spires of the various churches, the new six-story parking garage at the ferry dock, the glimmer of sunlight reflecting off the ocean. The wind was blowing toward the shore, so a faint stench of muck tinged the air. Directly beneath us was the Stantons' backyard, where an ancient garden swing creaked beneath a basswood tree.

"The beer cans are from the college students," said Pamella with indignation. "They throw them over the fence at night."

We stood side by side, arms resting on the wooden railing. The windblown hem of Pamella's sundress occasionally grazed my leg. "This is an amazing view," I said.

"You know what I really want?" she asked.

Here was the moment where I was supposed to say something suave, something simultaneously seductive and devil-may-care. "What?" I asked.

"One of those mega Christmas displays. Like in your father's store. That's what I want," she said. "When we lived on Long Island, there was this family, the Carranos, who owned a huge candy company—they were Italian *and* Jewish—and they always had these amazing displays. People drove all the way from Manhattan to see them. But you probably think that's stupid, don't you?" She was standing too close to me for my brain to function properly. Fortunately, the bells saved me: Episcopalians' and Congregationalists' and First Presbyterians' all peeling a simultaneous noon—albeit slightly out of sync.

"I could make you a display like that," I boasted.

"That would be *so* awesome," said Pamella. She squeezed the inside of my bare forearm—a fleeting warmth. "Let's go inside," she said.

She led me along the catwalk into the master bedroom, where her step-grandparents had once slept, then along a dimly-lit corridor to her own room. She'd already plastered the walls with posters for classic movies. *The Philadelphia Story*. *Breakfast at Tiffany's*.

The ceiling fixture consisted of four alabaster bowls, but two of the bulbs were burnt out. Or maybe there was a defect in the wiring. While I looked around, flicking the switches, Pamella told me about home-schooling, and accompanying her mom on tour, and about how nervous she was to start at Nathaniel Greene High School in September. I'd never heard anybody call it by its full name before. It was just "the high school." A crummy, third-tier high school at that. My dad had hoped to send me off to Andover or Choate or Billings Hall, but I hadn't wanted that, and neither had my mother, so we'd fought the "deportation order" until all of the deadlines had passed.

I mustered my courage. "It will be fine. I'll look after you," I said.

Pamella laughed. "Let's go downstairs," she said.

We found my father standing on the tabletop in the dining room. Dad had torn apart the garbage bag to cover the mahogany. He was brandishing a cordless drill in one hand and pressing the medallion into place with the other. "There," he said. He climbed down slowly, rubbed his bad knee, and packed up his toolbox.

"You were always so good at these things," said Sheila. "Like that time you fixed the trunk light in Papa's Cadillac. . . . It's so hard to believe that . . ." She didn't finish her sentence. She merely let her thoughts trail off, like a dying breeze, and escorted us to the door. Her step-daughter waved at me, grinning, from the edge of the dining room, but didn't follow us any farther. In seconds, we were trudging back down Banker's Hill. Alone. Already, I missed Pamella intensely.

I kicked a small stone along the pavement, hoping for an avalanche. It came to rest anemically beside a sewer grate. Dad asked, "Did I embarrass you by saying Sheila's daughter was pretty?"

"Can we talk about something else?"

"You should never feel ashamed of being attracted to a woman," he said. "You don't owe that to *anyone*."

We'd caught up with the small stone. I kicked it again. This time, it built momentum down that hillside. "Should I tell Mom that we were here?" I asked.

"Why shouldn't you?" Dad answered.

He didn't say anything else, after that, until we were back at the store. My mother's Plymouth Caravelle stood parked out front. She volunteered Mondays and Thursdays at the municipal library, but she'd taken off early to witness the SnoBlaster in action. Dad put his arm on the back of my neck, something he hadn't done since I was a little kid. "You know what?" he said. "Why don't you let me tell her?" And then he went inside and showed my mother how to make summer snow.

.....

Three days went by, a week. My father said nothing more of our visit to Sheila Stanton, and I didn't know whether he'd told my mother. I wasn't even sure what there was, really, to tell. Meanwhile, I inventoried our surplus from the previous Christmas season—everything from artificial aspen trees to the tiny "rice lights" designed for braiding into wreaths and kissing balls. Most had minute imperfections, but not the sort that Pamella would ever notice. I put off seeing her again, maybe because I feared she'd change her mind about the lights. About me. Instead, I stockpiled materials and drafted displays, some as elaborate as Rube Goldberg devices. I went to work each morning. I came home and fantasized about Pamella. I was totally self-absorbed. Soon enough, my father's secret—if it was that—drifted into the background.

"How are my two hard-working men?" my mother asked—on the second Tuesday after our hike up Banker's Hill. She had her face toward the gas range, where she was dropping batter-soaked vegetables into a frying pan. The kitchen smelled of grease and garlic. Each falling eggplant and zucchini produced a savory sizzle. I was struck by how heavy my mother looked bent over the oven—especially compared to bone-thin Sheila. "I'm trying something new," Mom said. "Patty-pan squash."

Dad rinsed and soaked his hands. An evening ritual. "Guess who I ran into the other day?" he said—a bit too nonchalant. "Sheila Stanton."

"Here in Creve Coeur?"

"She bought her parent's old place," said my father. "She had me install a chandelier for her."

Mom carried the plate of fried vegetables to the kitchen table. I piled twenty slices onto a paper napkin and gorged myself—not that I needed the calories. "It's funny," she said. "I hardly remember what she looks like."

"Terrific," said my father. "Honestly. Real good."

"Should I be worried?" teased my mother.

My father bristled abruptly. "Why should you be worried?"

"I was joking, Charlie. Heavens." My mother began scrubbing down the frying pan with Palmolive. "*Joking*."

"I know. Sorry. It's just, she's had such a hard time of it," said my father. "Wade's offered to put up a Christmas display for her stepdaughter. It might be a good experience for him."

"Because a future diplomat has to know about Christmas lights," said Mom—but her tone had turned mischievous again. Her own parents had operated a bowling alley in New London, Connecticut, and she was pleased with our quiet, middle-class existence, so *she* didn't mind me going into the lighting business. Why not?

"A future diplomat can always use a girlfriend," said my father. He tasted one of the fried vegetables and gave my mother a thumbs-up. She smiled. "I trust you won't worry too much," he said, "if I check up on him now and then."

"I'm done worrying," said my mother. "It makes me nervous."

Dad parted her bangs and kissed her on the forehead. "You've got *me*," he said. "All Sheila's got are holiday lights."

I'd never mentioned the Christmas display to my father, of course. He'd obviously paid the Stantons a second visit.

.....

The following afternoon, my father sent me back to the crime scene. "Go take some measurements. And forget about that surplus. We'll order everything custom fit," he commanded. But I didn't feel ready to see Pamella again—yet. Or maybe I wanted to, but at heart I was a coward. When I protested that August was way too early to plan a Christmas display, and besides, I was still 'on the clock,' Dad chuckled. "Sooner you start something," he said, "more time you have to undo your mistakes." So I hiked up Banker's Hill again, this time through an unseasonable fog. Sheila's stepdaughter opened the door. She appeared mildly surprised, but not unpleased, to see me.

Pamella wore a T-shirt with a torn shoulder and form-fitting pink sweatpants that must have doubled as sleepwear. She held a coffee mug in one hand. The entire entryway smelled of hot cocoa, and a thin residue of the beverage filmed her upper lip. I stood with one hand in my pocket, the other clenching the toolbox handle like a life buoy.

"I thought I'd drop by," I said, "to start on the Christmas lights."

"Oh. You really are going to do it," she said.

"I said I would, didn't I?" I said defensively. In my world, people did what they said they were going to do. Whether they wanted to or not. Here, needless to say, setting up this display was what I wanted most in the world. Or almost most.

All afternoon, I showed Pamella how to measure the heights of trees with an Abney clinometer and a leveling rod. We also jotted down the circumferences and the crown spreads, though these weren't essential. At first, I'd hoped Pamella might help me by calling out the readings on the measuring marker, signaling me in which direction to adjust the clinometer, as though hanging a painting. Eventually, I gave up on getting any meaningful assistance out of her. What she wanted to do was sit in the cool grass, sipping Hawaiian Fruit Drink from a miniature cardboard carton while watching me labor. When she got tired of doing nothing, she lugged out *The Complete Poetry of William Blake*, and read aloud. Tyger, tyger burning bright. "Like Deborah Kerr recites in *The End of the Affair*—after she breaks up with Van Johnson." I'd never heard of either of them. Or Blake. But this was Pamella's film obsession for the week, so I was more than willing to indulge her. By the time I actually got around to renting the movie—about an extramarital affair set in World War II London—Pamella had already moved on to a Katherine Hepburn film about a pet leopard.

My father showed up around four o'clock that first day, as he would many times over the subsequent months. He wore the same gray jacket, the same red suspenders, the same eight-hours growth of stubble. Sometimes, if he'd eaten a bagel and lox for lunch, tiny black poppy seeds remained wedged between his incisors. Yet there was no mistaking the newfound radiance in my father's eyes, the vigor in his step. Once, while simultaneously reviewing my calculations and explaining to Pamella the difference between A/C and D/C current, he'd started talking about opening a *second* showroom near the mall. In any case, he rarely spent much time inspecting my handiwork. Mostly, he stayed ten minutes with us, another twenty inside the house with Sheila Stanton, then he came back outside, glanced at his watch and announced it was time for us to depart. He was also prone to bursts of irritability, particularly on the ride home. In one instance, after Pamella told me her step-mom was directly descended from suffragette Elizabeth Cady Stanton, I asked my father where Grandpa Abe had come from in Europe. "How the hell should I know?" he snapped. "Who keeps track of these things, anyway?"

We kept up these afternoon visits all through August and then through September, long after the start of the school year. But we weren't the Stantons' only guests. In fact, for a woman who claimed she'd returned to Creve Coeur for "the peace and calm," Sheila kept a whirlwind of a social calendar. Some of her callers were from her life in the music industry: her agent; her accountant; an emaciated, one-eyed woman who sported a peacock-plumed hat and had apparently performed at Woodstock. But many of the men who spent time with Sheila—and most of the visitors *were* men—had a decidedly local flavor. There were a couple of fathers I recognized from Little League games; Old Mr. Decormier's son from the drugstore; the husband of one of my mother's bridge partners; a big, broad-shouldered guy with a limp. Some did household tasks for Sheila, like my Dad had done. Hoisting a piano. Painting shutters. Others just sat on the porch with her for half an hour, sipping iced tea. Several returned more than once. By the time my father arrived, around four o'clock, they were always long gone. I asked Pamella what this was about and she told me: Her stepmother was looking up all the friends she'd had in high school. "I hope *we're* still friends in twenty years," added Pamella, laughing. "Don't you think that would be awesome?" But Pamella had already proved herself far more popular at school than I would ever be—there was nothing particularly wrong with me, other than my weight, but also nothing particularly right—and often she went out with her new clique of friends while I labored alone on the lighting display.

Then, one afternoon in early October, my father pulled his van to the curbside an hour earlier than usual. It was snowing that day, an aftereffect of a Javanese volcanic eruption, the earliest recorded snowfall in Creve Coeur, in fact, since the Colonial Era—unless you counted Carl Pachinsky's feats with the SnoBlaster. The precipitation mixed with the dried leaves, and caked on paved surfaces as icy sludge. Pamella attempted to build a snowman, while I balanced on the slick gambrel roof, nailing quarter-inch hooks into the eaves at four-inch intervals. My father climbed the front steps just as Sheila Stanton and one of her guests stepped out onto the porch.

"Oh, Charlie," said Sheila. Surprised, I think.

"Hi," said my father. "I closed up early. The power went out."

"You remember Manny Standish," said Sheila. "From school."

"Manny the Pansy. Sure. The class behind me." The snow glistened off the top of my father's bald pate and the bridge of the other man's nose. "But I'll bet you're not Manny the Pansy anymore, are you?"

Manny sneezed twice. Then a third time. "No, Charles," he said. "I'm the headmaster at Billings Hall."

I feared the men might exchange punches. Instead, they shook hands.

"I should really get going," said my father. "I just wanted to give my boy a lift. Good to run into you, Manny. Dr. Standish, that is," he added. "Billings Hall is a damn fine school. Wade almost went there. Didn't you, Wade?"

"I missed the deadline," I called down.

"He's going to be a law professor," said my father.

Standish sneezed again and blew his nose into a cotton handkerchief.

In the van, I realized that my father was trembling. His entire body shook, all on account of this one brief encounter with the stiff, short, perpetually-allergic principal of a second-rate private school. Dad was still out-of-sorts, distracted and hostile, when we pulled into the driveway. In the kitchen, he scrubbed his hands. Then he dunked his entire head under the faucet. Tap water matted down his shirt.

"What's wrong?" pleaded my mother. "Charlie?"

"Nothing," said my father. "Or maybe everything. I ran into a guy I went to school with today and it upset me." He turned off the tap and dried his scalp with a dish towel. "Do you ever feel life is slipping through your fingers?" he asked—apropos of nothing. "That it's like snow. And every time you squeeze, it melts on you."

"I don't understand," said my mother. "Please, tell me. I *want* to understand."

"Like snow," said my father. "Like fucking snow." And that was all. It was the only time I can ever remember him speaking metaphorically.

.....

I continued to make progress on the Christmas display. My father let me spend as much money as I wanted, on whatever materials I wanted, so I ordered nine topiary reindeer and a four foot long Bethlehem sleigh. For the lead reindeer, I arranged a vermillion nose that lit up as one approached it. By mid-autumn, the lindens and sycamores in the Stanton yard had more mini-bulbs than leaves on them. Every crook in every branch was tightly wound with camouflaged electrical tape. I even designed a special series of grape and bell-pepper cluster lights that illuminated, sequentially, as visitors climbed the stairs, crossed the front porch, and then rang the doorbell. As they passed over the threshold, on the way out, a phalanx of incandescent lawn angels "played" *White Christmas* on twinkling harps. I did all of this myself, even hooking an auxiliary line into the main power cable—everything, except signing the official filings with the town. Either Dad or Carl Pachinsky had to do that, because I couldn't get my own electrician's license until I turned eighteen.

When the local media marked the twentieth anniversary of Sheila Stanton's rescue, bringing a rivulet of regional journalists back to the crime scene, one freelance reporter from Public Radio decided the lighting display was newsworthy. She asked for a short interview and a guided tour—although in the end, the piece never actually aired. But I remember how nervous she was, a girl just out of college, always gnawing at her hair when the recorder was off. She asked me: "What made you take on this project?" And I answered, cryptically, "It's a labor of love." But already I sensed that while I labored for love, the object of my love was losing interest in the display. Any given afternoon, the odds of me finding Pamella at home were less than 50-50, and she rarely returned from her outings before I departed. Wherever she went those evenings, and I guess I actively chose not to know, she never invited me along. When Halloween came, I was there alone on the porch to scare off the junior high school kids sporting plastic knives and red ribbons.

Meanwhile, my father was doing to the inside of the Stanton residence what I'd been doing to the outside: swamping it with expensive lighting. Every few days he appeared with yet another complimentary sample. A lamp filled with exotic seashells, or a dragonfly desk-light from Tiffany's, or a fluorescent music box that unfolded into a beveled mirror. First these were "housewarming gifts"; later, they were "to spruce the place up for the fall." He bought my mother more expensive gifts, too. Ruby earrings. An ermine wrap. "If we're not going to buy a sailboat," he said, "there's no point in socking all that cash away." But Mom never wore the jewelry, kept the stole in a box above her shoe shelf until it rotted. She made my father promise not to buy her anything else, and he didn't. But he kept digging up gifts for Sheila.

At the Stantons' house, Dad still glowed. Away from it, he grew less irritable, more morose. I'd wake up to use the bathroom at two in the morning, and he'd be sitting at the kitchen table, mindlessly stirring milk into a bowl of cornflakes. He went for long, aimless walks during the middle of the workday. He drove me out to the state fairgrounds on a whim to show me where he'd once eaten sixty jelly donuts in one sitting to impress a date. Presumably Sheila. He also drove me to Gates of Heaven Cemetery, north of Bristol, to show me where Grandpa Abe and Grandma Edith were buried.

Late one night, I heard my parents arguing in the kitchen. Or rather, my mother's voice, enraged, fraught, carrying up the stairs: "You're going to say she's had a hard time of it! Has it never crossed your mind that I'm having a hard time of it?" Then: "I don't care if it's nothing. I believe you, it's nothing. But it still *feels* like something." And then: "Why do I care if he hears me? He spends every waking moment over there anyway. Why don't you both just go live with the bitch and let me die in peace?"

.....

The next morning. In the van. My father turned on the news—Baby Jessica had just been rescued from the bottom of a well—then flipped to his oldies station. Dad's breath stank of coffee. He'd long ago Scotch-taped a family photograph to the dashboard, the three of us visiting the Vanderbilt Mansion at Newport, but I was suddenly struck by how much younger the man in the picture looked than the man at my side. His mustache had been entirely black then, his shoulders strapping. Far thinner and more handsome than I would ever be. It was hard to imagine the middle-aged retailer at my side, droning along to "Build Me Up, Buttercup," as the star southpaw pitcher who'd struck out seventeen straight Pawtucket Pirates for the Creve Coeur Heartbreakers. I rolled down the window, relishing the crisp autumn dawn.

"So how's your girlfriend?" Dad asked—without warning.

"I don't have a girlfriend."

"You know who I mean," he said. "Pamella with all those L's."

I stared out the window. "*I said*: I don't have a girlfriend."

"Well, what are you waiting for? When I was your age, I went out with a different girl every Saturday."

This was too much. "You can't do that anymore," I snapped. "Hell. What fucking planet do you live on?"

I knew he'd lay into me for cursing. I just didn't care. But then a Sheila Stanton song came on the radio, like a call to prayer, and he didn't say a thing.

.....

Something about this conversation with my father brought the anger inside me to a swift boil. All morning, while setting up a display of gooseneck and fleur-de-lis torchieres—modeled upon engravings of the Flavian Palace in Rome—I catalogued the ways in which Pamella Stanton had wronged me: the invitations to hang out with her clique that never arrived, the promises that we'd be friends forever. Every low-cut blouse she wore became an intentional effort to bait me, a calculated element in an elaborate plan of deception. Even her laughter was at fault. Like the music of the Sirens. My thoughts were so addled that I dropped a halogen bulb on the showroom floor. Less than two feet away from a customer wearing open-toed sandals. Then, clearing the shattered glass, I toppled an entire case of lava lamps. Five hundred dollars worth of merchandise. "Slippery fingers," said Carl Pachinsky. "Comes from jacking off too much." When he charged the broken fixtures against my paycheck, he included the sales tax.

On a different workday, I'd have had it out with Pachinsky. I hated him because he was fat and funny-looking, and crass, and he didn't care that he was fat and funny-looking and crass. I'd met his social-worker wife at a Memorial Day picnic, on the only occasion she'd ever come to a store event, and she was also fat and funny-looking—yet they'd seemed so damn happy together. Unreasonably happy. Nobody who looked like that had a right to happiness, as far as I was concerned. Not if I couldn't have Pamella. But I let the electrician dock my pay without complaining. Even he looked surprised. *It's not worth it*, I warned myself. *He'll be dead someday, and you'll have the last laugh*. I realized that my anger was like a land mine, capable of exploding only once. And I was determined to hoard the blast for my encounter with Pamella.

Dad kept me late at the store that afternoon. We'd received a shipment of pool-table lights one day too early—a wide assortment of French Quarter hanging counters, and Olympia billiard chandeliers, and Medici-style island lamps—and every last one of these needed to be inventoried before my father would sign the bill of lading. It was nearly dusk when I finally arrived at the crest of Banker's Hill.

I rang the doorbell. Nobody answered.

I figured Pamella was out with "friends"—whatever that really meant. But I intended to wait. I wandered around the side of the house, through the azalea hedge, looking for signs of activity in the windows. Nothing. Most of the curtains were drawn. The only illuminated light was an outdoor post lamp beside a drainpipe.

First I heard the creak of the garden swing and then I caught sight of her. A light gray shadow in a dark gray twilight. She called out my name.

"I didn't think you were home," I said.

As I approached, her body took shape. She sat wrapped in a man's raincoat—like Humphrey Bogart in the movies she'd urged me to watch. But the size of the coat made her appear small and vulnerable. Pamella was holding something in her hand. A can of soda. No—it was a can of beer. The remains of a six pack—only three cans left—rested beside her on the swing. "I came out here to think," she said.

"I've been thinking too . . ." I muttered.

She cut me off. "Sit down here next to me, Wade," she said. "Have a beer if you want to. It's Old Milwaukee, but that's all I could find."

I slid my index finger over the damp, peeling skin of the garden swing, but I didn't sit down. She handed me a beer—and I took it. Even though I'd never tasted one before. When I opened the tab, the sound punctured the darkness like a gunshot. I held the can in front of me, but didn't drink.

"Ma*ma*'s sick," said Pamella. Her voice was worn, joyless. "Really sick," she said. "She might die."

I felt a shiver cascade down my spine. All around us hung the electrical vines I'd laced into the foliage, dark and silent, yet capable of such brilliance. A raccoon lumbered in the yard—and I feared that it might claw out some of my wiring.

"I love you," I said.

Pamella's breath caught in her throat. The raccoon kept walking.

"You really do love me, don't you," she said. "Oh, Wade. You always know exactly the right thing to say." She reached over and squeezed by forearm, just as she'd done the day we first met. Her grasp was warm, but also clinical, almost like a nurse taking a pulse. And that—to quote the movie title—was the end of the affair.

. . . . .

Two days later, Sheila Stanton checked into Narragansett Bay Hospital for aggressive chemotherapy. Cancer of the lymph nodes. A particularly malignant variety. When I saw her next, propped on a pillow, surrounded by IV drips and gift baskets and the detritus of leftover hospital meals, she no longer looked female. She hardly appeared human. Her arms and legs were all bone. Skin draped off her clavicles like rumpled shirts off a hanger. But her face was broad and nearly jolly, swollen round by her medication. The fluorescent ceiling lights—two rectangular cloud panels—tinted her jaundiced skin a sickly yellow-violet. Every day, after work, my father sat with Sheila Stanton until the nurse shift changed at the end of visiting hours. Now, he made no effort to conceal these visits from my mother.

My parents argued every evening, every morning over breakfast. Even my presence no longer tamed their hostility. But the worst of it was late at night, after I was in bed, when my father tried to watch television, and my mother yanked out the cord.

"You don't owe that to her," Mom insisted. "She's the one who ran off and abandoned you. Not the opposite."

"Under particularly extenuating circumstances," answered my father. "I don't owe it to her. I owe it to *me*."

"Because you're in love with her," my mother shouted. "Because you're having an affair with her."

I could hear Dad plugging the television back into the wall. Sometimes Ted Koppel or Johnny Carson blared out at top volume. "Jesus, Gwen. She's terminally ill," said my father—in a way that sounded more like a confession than a denial.

Several times, my father brought me with him to visit Sheila. First at the hospital in Cranston, later at a special facility for cancer patients. She had many other visitors too—even Manny Standish and his plain, gray-haired wife—but Dad didn't seem to care anymore. He'd step out of the room until they left and then return to sit at Sheila's bedside. Sometimes, he read to her from the *Providence Journal* or *People Magazine* or a popular history of the Soviet Union by a man named Lev Byokov. All about Stalin's 5-Year Plans and the purging of Lavrentiy Beria. I doubt he understood a word. Usually, he just sat. Or sat and held her limp hand. Pamella was always there too. Mostly alone. But once she brought along a tall, lanky high school senior named Nicholas whom she introduced as her boyfriend. Without a hint of shame. Or even hesitation. As though it were perfectly natural for her boyfriend and me to get along socially. But the worst part was that he was actually a pretty decent guy. When he and Pamella were ready to leave—he was tutoring her in trigonometry—he even offered me a lift across town.

After that, I stayed away. I concentrated all of my energy on the Christmas display, somehow clinging to those electrical cords as my only remaining hope with Pamella. Sheila called me her "personal electrician" and let me have her front door key. That gave me easy access to the circuit-breakers and the switching cables in the cellar.

My father picked me up in the van each night on the way back from the hospital.

"Is she really going to die?" I asked him.

"I hope not," he said. "She has very good doctors."

I sensed that was my father's way of saying her check was cashed. Sooner, rather than later. But Thanksgiving arrived, and my father brought Sheila cutlets and dark meat from our turkey, and she didn't give up. By the second week of December, she was promenading through the hospice corridors with the help of a walker. Her hair started growing back in random patches. One day, according to my Dad, she put on lipstick. Her recently terminal disease entered a state of spontaneous remission. Not a cure, certainly. But also not imminent death. Sheila grew restless away from home and made plans to leave the hospice on Christmas Eve. Up to then, she'd taken little interest in my lighting project, or in me, for that matter, but now she suddenly wanted to see the first demonstration of the lighting display. Sheila went so far as to summon me to her hospice room and to make me promise not to start the show without her. She wanted to "flick the switch"—in her words—like she'd once done with the New Year's Ball in Times Square. I tried to explain to her that this wasn't like that, that lighting her yard required numerous switches adjusted over a matter of hours, but she wouldn't hear anything of it. "You're a professional electrician," she said. "Make it all into one switch." So I did.

That Christmas Eve brought one of the worst ice storms in recent memory, a fitting conclusion to a year of wacky weather. Frost several inches thick built up on exposed surfaces, petrifying the tree branches to rock. (The water weight would eventually take down most of my elaborate wiring.) But Christmas lights or no Christmas lights, Sheila Stanton insisted upon returning home. She phoned our house—something she'd never done before—and point blank asked my father for a lift. He told her that he'd come for her after supper. Mom threw a tantrum. She'd worked all afternoon preparing a pre-Christmas feast of goose and poached salmon. "Go spend Christmas with Sheila Stanton," she shouted. And she tossed my father's meal—glass plate and all—onto the glazed lawn.

So my father picked up Sheila Stanton at the hospital. They made it as far as the turnoff for Route One, just north of the 3-Mile Bridge. The Kissing Bridge, they used to call it back then. Because a politician named Kissing had once jumped off it. The telephone poles were down across the roadway, and my father set about removing them with the greatest of care. Avoiding the power lines. Rolling the wood posts to the embankment. He did the job in under twenty minutes.

On the way back to his delivery truck, he stepped into a puddle—the residue of ice melted by the exhaust from the vehicle. The live wire at the other end instantly drove thirty-three thousand volts of electricity up his legs and into his body.

.....

It was Sheila Stanton who phoned my mother to tell her that my father was dead. And four hours later, it was Sheila who, while Mom and I waited at an emergency roadblock after an embankment gave way on the interstate, identified his corpse for the deputy coroner. When we finally did arrive at the hospital, bone-tired, iced-through, broken, there was nothing to do but wait for the storm to pass. Sheila was also waiting—for an ambulance to take her back to Banker's Hill. She offered my mother her sympathy. Mom nodded—that was the most civility she could muster—and looked away.

My father's funeral was far larger than he ever could have imagined. Lighting wholesalers came from up and down the Eastern seaboard. Also his associates from Little League, from the P.T.A., from the Friends of the Creve Coeur Public Library. Dying young has a way of drawing a crowd. My old nemesis, Carl Pachinsky, wore a dark three piece suit and sunglasses—looking something like a beached cartoon sea mammal without his trademark coveralls. Pachinsky's wife brought a get well card my father had written her after her disc surgery, and passed it around. It was a cold, windy day, with dark clouds streaked across the horizon.

After the service, mourners circled around my mother and me to offer their condolences. Others, particularly those who had known my father many years earlier, formed a similar, if smaller, conclave around Sheila and her stepdaughter. What exactly they said to her, I don't know. But her expression remained hard and distant through the morning, not the face of a woman who'd lost a lover. Nor did Pamella look like she'd lost a surrogate father. They were like a pair of stones that morning, hand in hand, inseparable, watching us with the uneasy relief of near-strangers passing perilously close to another family's calamity.

Scouting for the Reaper

Nothing sells tombstones like a Girl Scout in uniform. This was my father's pearl of entrepreneurial genius, the closest he ever came to a formal business plan, and it's how I ended up lugging thirty pounds of granite onto Delia Braithwaite's front porch, while sporting a pleated skirt, a collared blouse and a trefoil pin. "You make your profit on the 'his-and-hers' specials," Papa coached—referring to deals that allow surviving spouses to lock in future epitaphs at present-day rates. "Who's a grieving widow going to trust on a twofer? A family man? Or a slick-talking bachelor?" So at the age of eight—when my sister Katie entered high school—I'd inherited both the job and the outfit, and five years later, Papa was still introducing me to potential clients as his *eleven-year-old* beauty. It didn't matter that, unlike my sisters, I'd never actually been a Girl Scout. Or that my chest had outgrown my hand-me-down jade green vest.

Delia Braithwaite had been my father's first wife. They'd married when Papa was studying marble-work in Copenhagen and split up soon after he'd inherited the monument shop in Yonkers from Grandpa Melvin. Ten stormy months, no kids, no strings. I doubt he'd ever expected to see her again, and I'm sure he never imagined that, at fifty, he'd be ringing the doorbell of her privet-shrouded Scarsdale estate to pitch her a deluxe gravesite. But there he was, bogus Girl Scout in tow. It was a mild Saturday afternoon in late April and the heady aroma of hyacinths had triggered Papa's allergies. He sneezed repeatedly into his handkerchief, his thick neck bulging. A stylish, svelte woman in a velvet cheetah bodysuit opened the door.

"Gordon?" she asked—hesitantly, as much to herself as to us. "*Gordon,*" she responded, more confidently, welcoming, as though answering her own question. Then: "Gordon, Gordon, Gordon." Shaking her head. As in: *Well, it's about time*. Or: *Look what the dog dug up*. She was conducting an entire conversation just by repeating Papa's name. "*So*, Gordon?" she demanded. "Aren't you going to *say* anything?"

"Hello, Delia," said Papa. "You haven't changed one bit."

"Nonsense," exclaimed our hostess. "I look like I'm old enough to be my own grandaunt. Like Whistler's mother! But it can't be helped, can it?" She turned toward me without warning, when I'd nearly forgotten that I was physically present in her entryway, and not merely watching a theatrical performance, and she asked, "And who might *this* be?"

Papa didn't allow me a chance to answer. "That's Natalie. My eleven year old beauty," he said. "We've come straight from Junior Scouts."

"*Natalie,*" echoed Delia Braithwaite. But she said *my* name only once. "I've got a seventeen year old of my own around here somewhere," she added, shrugging. "He'll turn up when you least expect him." Then she led us across the foyer, walking with a pronounced limp, and resting her weight on a wooden cane.

Every object in the room demanded attention: the cut-glass and ormolu chandelier, the Comtoise clock at the foot of the spiral staircase, a black-and-white tiled floor worthy of Vermeer.

Yet most striking were the numerous glazed sculptures, on every ledge and tabletop, depicting abstract nudes in various states of embrace. I guessed that this was Delia Braithwaite's own handicraft. My father glanced up the stairs, drawing a long whistle under his breath. I rested the sample case against the wainscoting.

"Henry isn't here," said Delia. "I didn't see the point in that."

This jolted Papa back to the task at hand. "My sincerest condolences, Delia," he offered.

"Condolences? For what?"

Delia Braithwaite appeared genuinely surprised. My father, looking equally puzzled, toyed clumsily with his large hands.

"I just thought..." he stammered. "You wanted a headstone, didn't you?"

"Oh, the *headstone*." Delia grinned. "The headstone is for *me*."

.....

Papa had been in the carving yard alongside the house when Delia Braithwaite phoned. He was hunched over his outdoor workbench, his overalls caked in quartz dust, etching on a rubber stencil with a utility scalpel. While he labored, he bellowed show tunes in his warm, Bronx-inflected baritone. *Oh What a Beautiful Mornin'*. *Some Enchanted Evening*. I lay sunning myself atop a boulder that overlooked the conclave of unfinished headstones, engrossed in a pocket romance novel that I'd concealed inside my school-issued copy of *Middlemarch*. Katie perched nearby atop a rusted swing, playing tic-tac-toe in the dust with her boot. She was listening for the nasal blast of her boyfriend's Mustang, dreamy-eyed like a girl who knows she'll be kissed before sundown. Orioles and grackles thrashed in the crabapple thicket that separated our property from the municipal duck pond, punctuated by the honking of taxis on Waterloo Avenue, and the rumble of eighteen wheelers passing on the interstate. Suddenly, the telephone rang in the kitchen, livid as a fire alarm. A moment later, my mother emerged through the screen door with the portable receiver pressed against her shoulder.

"*Gor*-don!" she cried. Her voice, once the finest soprano in local summer stock, had grown perpetually louder as her hearing deteriorated. "Te-le-*phone!*"

My father stopped singing. He dried the sweat from his hands slowly, unwilling to be rushed by the caller. Then he took a swig of iced tea from his canteen and lumbered across the yard—his gait as steady as a gunslinger's.

"It's *Delia,*" announced Mama, inquisitive, her eyebrows raised. She'd shaded the name with a hint of distaste, as though retrieving a soiled napkin between her fingertips. "For *you.*"

Papa walked the telephone to the far end of the veranda. He spoke for the better part of five minutes, pausing to scribble a note, most likely the caller's address, while my mother hovered on the nearby steps, periodically grimacing or rolling her eyes. After he snapped off the phone, they conferred briefly. Then my father brushed aside Mama's gray-tinged bangs, kissed her on the forehead, and climbed back down into the yard.

"Natalie!" Papa called. "Put on your uniform! We're making a house call!"

"What do you need Natalie for?" demanded Mama. "Jesus, Gordon. You're not planning to swindle your own ex-wife?"

The word 'swindle' was a surefire way to rankle Papa. Now, he couldn't back down. "My ex-wife is a rich woman," he snapped. "And since when are *you* so concerned about Delia?"

I'd never heard of Delia before. I knew nothing of the first marriage.

Mama scowled. She'd given Papa hell for "exploiting" us girls ever since he'd first dragged Annie on a sales call—but only when she was upset about something else. Usually, she didn't mind the extra sales, the cash for dinners out or weekends at Cape May. "You already know what I think," she said, her voice fraught with injury, and she disappeared into the house, letting the screen door slam shut angrily behind her.

Papa appeared unfazed. "Let's get a move on, Natalie," he ordered.

I looked to Katie for help—for illumination, for pity—but she wouldn't meet my gaze, so I darted inside, stashed my romance novel under my mattress, and changed into my undersized uniform. On impulse, I left off the wool beret and itchy nylon tights.

My father stood waiting for me in the garage, reviewing the inventory in his sample cases. Mama—I knew from many years of careful observation—would be upstairs, moping beneath a heap of afghan quilts and down comforters. "Jealousy is an ugly thing. Like a crack in healthy marble," Papa said. "Your mother is very lucky that I love her as much as I do."

I said nothing. I felt embarrassed for both of us, and for Mama too, as though I'd interrupted the pair of them having sex.

We walked out to the truck. On the drive into Westchester County, Papa told me all that he believed I needed to know about his relationship with Delia Braithwaite: that they'd apprenticed together under Lars Willumsen in Denmark, that he hadn't laid eyes on her in thirty years, that he and Mama had never mentioned her because she wasn't relevant to their lives. *Or mine.* "She's relevant only because she's married to the CEO of Braithwaite & Nolan," he added. "To you, she's just a wealthy woman in the market for a headstone. Okay?"

I nodded.

"Good," said Papa.

He popped a cassette into the tape deck. Soon we were listening to Robert Preston seduce Marion the Librarian, leaving Mama's displeasure far behind us. The overhead sun coaxed figments of water from the parched asphalt. We'd already advanced forty minutes up the parkway when Papa turned to me, surprised, and demanded, "Where's your funny hat?"

.....

"Do you know what the problem with dying is?" asked Delia.

She'd steered us into a brightly-lit parlor furnished entirely in white. Above the mantel hung an enormous canvas swathed with blue rectangles, yellow crescents, crimson crosses and sinuous green lines—as though the painting had sucked all the color from the rest of the room. The work may well have been a Kandinsky. Again, abstract lovers—some stone, some aluminum—caressed on the coffee table and atop a mahogany stand beside the bay windows. Delia Braithwaite had poured us each a tall glass of sweetened pink lemonade from a crystal pitcher. Then she'd settled down far too close to me on the sofa.

When Papa failed to reveal the *real* problem with dying, she patted my thigh and asked, "How about *you*, young lady? Do *you* know what the problem with dying is?"

"Maybe you're not really dying," I suggested. "Maybe you'll get better."

"You sound just like my husband," said Delia. "Henry is always going on about the miracles of modern science, insisting that they'll find a cure. But that's a pipe dream. Let's face it: If they didn't find a cure for Lou Gehrig, they're certainly not going to find one for me." Our hostess laughed—a lush, rising laugh like a waltz up a staircase. I'd met dying people before—Great Aunt Arlene in the nursing home, the chain-smoking Moroccan who co-owned the flower shop where Mama worked—but none had ever seemed so happy. "I'll tell you what the *real* problem with dying is," Delia said, her eyes fixed on Papa. "It's a one-shot deal. You don't have an opportunity to learn from your mistakes."

My father remained stone-faced. He sat with one leg crossed over the opposite knee, nursing his lemonade like cognac. "I'm sorry you have to go through this," he said.

"Me too," agreed Delia. "I've been making a list of the things I'd still like to do. Photographing the Serengeti, picnicking beneath the Colossi of Memnon, making love on Easter Island in the shadows of the moai. Not that I'm actually going to do *any* of that—but it's nice to have fantasies. And daydreaming keeps me busy, now that I can't sculpt." I blushed. I wasn't used to discussing love-making fantasies, however tame, during casual conversation. Delia set her empty glass on the coffee table. "I also wanted to see *you*, Gordon. You don't mind my saying that, do you? It's rather convenient that you sell tombstones for a living, isn't it?"

"You didn't always think that," said Papa.

"No, I suppose I didn't," agreed Delia. "You never let anything slide, do you?"

"I just call things as they are," answered Papa. "Or, at least, as I see them."

This sort of cryptic aggression was nothing like the father I knew—but neither was having a clandestine ex-wife. I longed to leap from the sofa and retreat to the safety of the truck. Instead, I spread an embroidered cloth across the tabletop and started to lay out the granite samples: small rectangles in coral gray and sierra white, Wausau red and Salisbury pink, each carved with R.I.P. in uncial gothic. Papa often told clients how Great Grandma Pauline had hand-stitched the cloth in the days when Great Grandpa Leo went door-to-door on horseback. A reminder that Luftigs had been hawking headstones since 1892. (Mama, who'd actually bought the cloth from a discount bin at Gimbels, would *not* have been amused.) I focused on adjusting and readjusting the tiny stones, afraid of making eye contact with Delia Braithwaite.

"So how have *you* been, Gordon? How have you *really* been?" she asked. "I do hope you've had a good thirty years."

"I have, Delia," answered Papa. His tone was matter-of-fact and unequivocal, which is what a daughter wants to hear. It didn't cross my mind—not until later—that he might have been lying. "Now tell me, Delia, what exactly are you looking for in the way of a stone?"

Our hostess appeared disappointed, irked—either by Papa's thirty good years or his change of subject. Her eyes settled on the sample display. I felt suddenly unwelcome.

"I have absolutely no idea," she answered "Honestly, I thought you'd tell me. Like I said, Gordon, I've never done this before . . ."

"That's why I've brought samples," said Papa.

I knew what came next: My father's sermon on how headstones were like houses, each suited to a particular taste and temperament. The sound of a barking dog, followed by a door slamming in the entryway, cut him short. Seconds later, a deep masculine voice announced, "Rodin caught another goddam squirrel," and then the speaker sauntered into the room. He was a broad-shouldered, square-jawed teenage dreamboat with a playful smile and long, golden-saffron bangs that nearly concealed his eyes. When he realized that Delia had company, he said, "Oh, hi," sheepishly, waving toward us, and his cheeks blossomed like peonies. Only then did I notice his vacant, irregular gaze—and the collapsible white cane tucked under one muscular arm: My newfound Adonis was blind.

"This is my wayward son, Lucien," said Delia. "And this is Gordon Luftig. He's selling me a tombstone."

"Delia—" Lucien objected, calling his mother by her first name.

Delia cleared her throat audibly, her means of staring him down—akin to my own mother's icy, '*we have company*' look. "And this is his eleven-year-old daughter. Natasha, right?"

"Natalie," I mumbled.

"I was a scout when *I* was eleven," said Delia Braithwaite, "as hard as *that* is to believe."

Our hostess placed her right hand on her heart and declaimed:

> *"On my honor, I will try:*
> *To serve God and my country,*
> *To help people at all times,*
> *And to live by the Girl Scout Law."*

"Not bad for a dying woman, is it?" she asked.

I despised Delia Braithwaite for informing Lucien that I was eleven. As the ugliest thirteen year old in the eighth grade, I had little shot at dating him—even if he couldn't see me through his own eyes. Somehow, he was bound to find out how hideously unattractive I was. Yet branded an eleven year old *child*, I wouldn't even have an opportunity to fail.

If my father was surprised by Lucien's lack of vision, he didn't let on.

"I was just showing your mother some samples," said Papa. "I think it's best to choose your coloring first and *then* decide upon a suitable design."

"You have an awful lot of samples, don't you?" asked Delia. "What's this one?"

She scooped up a pink-hued specimen.

"Sunset pink," observed Papa. "Very eye-catching. The deep pinks have a mystical look to them . . . and a striking reflection when polished to a high sheen."

Delia returned the stone to its original place like a puzzle piece.

"I need an epitaph, don't I?" she declared. "How do I want to be remembered?"

"That's entirely for you to decide," Papa replied patiently. "Many people prefer to purchase a stone and then choose an inscription later."

"That makes no sense at all," snapped Delia. "How can I decide what stone I want if I don't know what I'm writing on it?" She clasped her hands together, her posture rigid. "Form follows function, doesn't it? So what do you think, Lucien? What wisdom should your mother leave behind for eternity?"

"I think you should concentrate on living," said Lucien.

"How about you, Natasha?" asked Delia. "Any ideas?"

I did have a choice phrase or two, considering that she'd butchered my name *again*—but not ones that I dared express. She was my future mother-in-law, after all. (I'd already decided that I was going to marry Lucien Braithwaite, or that I would die a virgin trying.) My future husband was half-sitting on the back of the sofa, his strapping forearms folded across his chest, so close to me that I could have touched his bare elbow.

"I suppose you should come back again, Gordon. How about next Saturday?" asked Delia—but it was more an order than a question. She rose from the sofa with the help of the cane and dusted the upholstery lint from her bodysuit. "I'm sure I'll come up with something by then. Maybe I can find something on the Internet."

Our hostess led us through the oak-paneled dining room into the opulent foyer, dragging her weak leg like an anchor. Lucien followed in silence, feeling his way deftly along the walls. He even paused at one point to straighten a picture frame. I felt deathly self-conscious watching him, although I knew he couldn't see me. When Delia waved goodbye to us, my dreamboat stood behind her like a bodyguard.

Farewell Lucien, I thought. Farewell, my darling.

He smiled at us and shut the heavy door.

I stood at the curbside, smitten, pollen-drenched, already mapping out the hours until the coming weekend, while Papa hoisted the sample case onto the bed of the truck. "Your mother is not going to be a happy camper," he said. He wiped his swollen eyes and climbed into the cab. I followed. "I suppose this is a good life-lesson for you, Natalie," he said. "Cracked marble isn't pretty, but sometimes it can't be helped." I should have been alarmed by Papa's meditative tone—but I was far too love-struck to care.

.....

Mama met the truck at the head of the cul-de-sac. She was wearing her threadbare terrycloth robe, her short hair damp and tussled, pacing between sidewalk and street like a madwoman walking an imaginary dog. Twilight had already fallen, casting lazy shadows off the telephone poles and the heads of the crabapples—the mild spring evening somehow accentuating my mother's fury. I couldn't help comparing her broad features and childbearing hips to Delia's classical, hard-edged beauty. Mama, even in her heyday, had merely displayed the fleeting, girlish charms of a well-fed peasant. She hardly gave my father a chance to climb down from the truck before she launched her first salvo.

"Well?" she demanded.

"She couldn't make up her mind about the lettering," said Papa, trying to sound indifferent. "She wants us back again next weekend."

"I have a suggestion," snapped Mama. "How about: *Here lies a cold-hearted bitch.*"

"Can you please watch your language, Eileen? For heaven's sake." My father scanned the neighbors' homes, their brightly-lit windows slicing through the dusk. He unloaded the heavier sample case, leaving the other for me, and lugged it up the driveway. "If it's *that* important to you, Eileen, I won't go back. I'll cancel the whole thing." Papa set the case down beside the garage door and added dryly, "It's not as though we could use the money."

"That's *so* not the point. I don't want you to *not* go back," Mama retorted. "I just don't want you to forget how that woman treated you. How she discarded you like a broken sculpture, like an animal carcass, like a piece—"

"Believe me, I haven't forgotten," said my father. "And it wasn't all that simple."

Mama's fist pounded the air. "How wasn't it that simple?"

My father stepped toward her and gently peeled open her clenched hand. "Let's not fight about this, okay?" he pleaded. "Look, life has more than caught up with her. She's dying of ALS and,"—here my father lowered his voice—"she's married to a first-rate asshole."

"Did you meet him?"

"I didn't need to," Papa answered. "Trust me. I can tell."

"Well, he's a rich asshole. Better than a . . ."

"Better than a *what*?" asked Papa.

They faced each other in silence, dwarfed by the hulking shadow of the unlit house.

"Nothing," said Mama. She leaned her body into my father's chest, and he wrapped his arms around her. "I'm sorry. I just hate her for what she did to you."

"If Delia hadn't discarded me like—what was that?—an animal carcass, I wouldn't have a beautiful wife and three brilliant daughters, now would I?" asked Papa. "Besides, she's been dealt a pretty lousy hand. She's got a blind kid, too. I'm sure that's punishment enough."

"Serves her right," said Mama. "I hope she catches it."

I wanted to gouge their eyes out for calling Lucien a punishment. Instead, I retreated to my bedroom and buried my head in the pillows. I could hear Katie and her boyfriend making out in the converted attic, the springs of her Murphy bed dancing above my ceiling, and I pretended that they were actually us, Lucien and I, and that he'd torn open my pleated jade skirt and I was guiding his powerful hands through the perpetual darkness.

.....

The next seven days lasted several millennia. I drew a grid containing one hundred sixty-eight boxes, for each intervening hour, and crossed them off one by one. I watched the second hand on the dining room clock making its glacial rounds. I was consumed with the dread that some unforeseen obstacle would interpose itself between me and my impending encounter with Lucien—that he might step in front of a locomotive or elope to Reno with the blind cheerleader who'd been profiled in the county newspaper. My concern may seem rather excessive, considering that Lucien Braithwaite and I had hardly exchanged two sentences. But for a lonely, flat-chested thirteen-year-old girl nicknamed Dumbo, on account of her arresting ears, the prospect of intimacy can become all consuming. I yearned for a chance to reinvent myself, away from the unforgiving corridors of Samuel Tilden Middle School, and a handsome blind boy offered a once-in-an-adolescence opportunity. I was so anxious, so fragile, that even the sight of a baby rabbit on the lawn sent me bawling.

Mama was also on edge. Our family dinners, which had grown increasingly subdued ever since Annie had escaped on scholarship to Vassar and Katie had absented herself psychologically from the household, suddenly became ground zero in the one-sided verbal war between my mother and her predecessor. "I've got the perfect epitaph, Gordon," declared Mama. "How's this? *Went Digging for Gold.*" On another night, she suggested: *"Delia Luftig Braithwaite: She Married Up."* Mama couched her jealousy in the guise of righteous indignation at how Delia had once treated Papa. This helped me piece together the details of the divorce: How my father had felt obliged to return to Yonkers, to support Grandma Florence and Great Grandma Pauline and Uncle Lester, who was only a toddler when Grandpa Melvin collapsed, while Delia had been determined to remain in Denmark. She'd married an avant-garde sculptor, a protégé of Willumsen, an artistic heir to the late Dietrich Marcus. Grave dealing hadn't been part of the bargain. Delia was more than willing to support Papa on the allowance provided by her own father, a Park Avenue urologist, but she felt no obligation toward poor relations whom she'd never even met. So they parted. Not *un*-amicably. Yet now, three decades later, Mama declared the woman's disloyalty unpardonable. She compared her, at various times, to Judas Iscariot and Lady Macbeth and Lord Haw Haw. Papa let these outbursts take their course. He never defended Delia. Instead, he'd deflect Mama's sarcasm with an intimate gesture—a squeeze of the wrist, a kiss on the palm—and he'd say, "I dodged a bullet with that woman, didn't I?"

My father's reunion with Delia had affected him, too. I know this because one evening, while I was concealed in the arbor, reading an antebellum-era romance with a flashlight and fantasizing about Lucien, Papa exited the house by the kitchen stairs and climbed down to his workbench. But he didn't pick up where he'd left off, lettering "R.I.P. Chester the Schnauzer" onto a granite doghouse while singing *If I Were A Rich Man*. He didn't even touch his tools. Instead, he stood motionless with his hands in his pants pockets, his broad shoulders slightly hunched, and stared at the unfinished gravestone, almost *through* it, as though it were his own. I don't know if he was thinking of his relationship with Delia—or merely of the reality that she was dying. *That a woman he'd once loved would soon no longer exist*. He stood in the damp twilight for nearly an hour, and I felt a sudden urge to hug him, and to apologize for being such a disappointing daughter, for not wearing my nylon tights and wool beret with greater alacrity, but of course I didn't do that. So Papa retreated up the kitchen stairs again, slowly, wearily.

And then it was Saturday.

.....

Delia Braithwaite greeted us from a plaid beach chair on her front yard. She'd traded her cheetah bodysuit for a loosely-draped silk robe; her long chestnut hair was looped around a pair of knitting needles. The wooden cane rested against a tall stack of nearby books, and in her lap she held a bowl of fresh cherries, which she offered first to Papa and then to me. "How's Scouts, Natasha?" Delia asked. She held up three fingers in solidarity. I raised three fingers of my own, while sliding my other arm into my tights to scratch. Then I remembered that I was supposed to offer my *opposite* hand for the Girl Scout shake—Katie, who'd once cared deeply about these details, had warned me countless times—but my partner had already turned away.

"I've been hunting for an epitaph all week, Gordon," said Delia, "but I'm afraid I haven't made much progress. When you search for epitaphs on the Internet, you come up with lots of psalms and sappy poetry, but nothing you can actually use." She retrieved her reading glasses from the apron of her robe and flipped open the topmost book on the stack. "I figured I'd find something in the *Golden Treasury of American Verse*, but the only potential lines even remotely tolerable were Ogden Nash—'Candy is dandy, but liquor is quicker'—and when I told Henry, he threatened to have me buried in an unmarked grave." Our hostess snapped shut the poetry anthology decisively; it struck me that her husband had said no such thing. "What do you think, Gordon? 'Candy is dandy, but liquor is quicker'? Or how about something simple and barebones like 'Beloved ex-wife and mother'?"

Papa's face remained impassive as a bed sheet. He reached toward Delia as though to reassure her with a gentle squeeze of her shoulder—part of his routine with female customers—but, at the last moment, he stuffed his hand into his pants pocket. "All I can do is offer up suggestions, Delia," he said. "In the end, it's your choice. That being said, you can rest assured that nearly everyone manages to find something that they're comfortable with."

"I suppose you don't get many long term complaints."

"Emily Dickinson is often a popular choice," continued my father, "especially among educated woman. Or *you* might like a quotation about sculpting."

"What I'd *like*," answered Delia, "is to have Lana Turner's teenage body. But we're past what I'd *like*, Gordon. *Well past*. At this point, it's more a matter of what I'd settle for."

"In that case," replied my father, deadpan, "I suppose many educated women settle for a quotation from Emily Dickinson."

"Okay, Gordon. Have your fun," Delia fired back. "You'll only have a few chances left to mock Delia Braithwaite, so you might as well make the most of them. The neurologists—in case you care—say I'm down to my final eighteen months. Not that anybody *around here* believes them. Henry and Lucien are both practically drowning in denial. How does this sound for an epitaph? 'I told you I was sick!'"

Our hostess was *flirting*. She was dying and bitter *and* she was flirting. I scanned the corners of the lawn, hoping for a glimpse of my future husband, but a morbid torpor hung over the manicured facades of rhododendron and forsythia. The house was equally still, a colossal ranch-style tomb. No sign of Lucien. The only evidence of life beyond our own was, drifting from some distance past the house and across the Braithwaite's red clay tennis courts, the deep, playful bark of a large dog. Fortunately, my presence must have made Delia as uneasy it made me, because she turned suddenly in my direction and said, "Why don't you go find Lucien, Natasha? He should be out back with Rodin." I didn't need to be told twice. Yet even as I darted toward my unwitting fiancé, following the pachysandra-lined footpaths and ducking through a lilac-wrapped arbor, I was seized with an unpleasant realization regarding my future late mother-in-law: Delia was butchering my name *intentionally*, because she found doing so amusing. She knew damn well that I was Natalie, not Natasha. She didn't care.

.....

I found Lucien beside the swimming pool, counting push-ups on the concrete. He'd stripped down to his boxer shorts, and perspiration glistened off his shoulder blades, off the caps of his muscular shoulders, off the nape of his sun-bronzed neck. The dog, a black Labrador, stood exhausted and dripping atop a vinyl-matted chaise-longue. In the deep end of the water, a Frisbee drifted like a raft. I stood motionless, hoping Rodin would ignore me, watching electrified as Lucien's biceps contracted and released. When he reached fifty, his breath grew shorter. He paused at seventy-five, grunted his way from eighty to ninety. "One-fucking-hundred," he announced, falling flat on his stomach. Then he stood up and, glancing toward me, warned, "Didn't anybody ever tell you not to sneak up on blind people in their underwear?"

I didn't move. I didn't speak. I wanted to sink into the earth forever.

"Hey, Natalie. You better say something before I sick Rodin on you."

Lucien flashed his teeth. He wiped the sweat from his underarms with a crimson bath towel. My eyes focused on the small horizontal scar at the flank of his abdomen where he'd apparently had his appendix removed, a mark nearly identical to my own. I considered running back to the truck and locking myself inside.

"How did you know it was me?"

"Your shampoo," he answered.

I drew one of my bangs to my nose. I could hardly smell anything. Maybe a hint of citrus flavor and another vaguely toxic scent.

"I *like* the smell," he added. "It's sweet."

Lucien tossed the towel onto the chaise-longue. He clapped his hands together and Rodin sprang to attention. "Frisbee! Go get it, boy!" cried Lucien, dispatching the dog into the water at top speed. "He's not a guide dog, just an old-fashioned mutt," my future husband explained. "But nobody knows that, so I take him into the post office . . . and even into upscale restaurants. Who's ever going to tell a blind guy that his dog's not the *right kind* of dog?"

"I had my appendix removed too," I blurted out. "When I was eight."

Lucien traced his fingers along his scar. "And you're eleven now, right? So that was three years ago. I had mine out three years ago too. New Year's Eve." He eased the Frisbee from Rodin's jaw and lobbed it back into the pool, only inches from where it had been. "We were skiing up in Vermont and my girlfriend had to drive me to the hospital through a blizzard."

No physical pain had ever hurt me so badly. *Even Lucien had a girlfriend.*

"You're wondering about the skiing, aren't you?" he asked. "They have a special course fitted out with ropes. I'm actually ranked seventeenth in the country. I've got a shot at the Special Olympics in three years."

I sensed my anger mounting. *How could he think I cared about skiing?*

"Is your girlfriend from Westchester?" I asked.

"Originally. Janine graduated last spring," said Lucien. "She's at school in Colorado. It's a really good program for psychology. I was going to go out there too . . . for skiing . . . but now with Delia the way she is, I don't know *what* I'm going to do. I still have another month to decide . . . almost six weeks . . ."

He turned his head away, as though gazing at the horizon, although obviously he couldn't see it. His damaged eyes looked moist—or I may have imagined this. I longed to hug him, to plant butterfly kisses on his eyelashes, but I didn't dare.

"I'm sorry about your mother," I said.

"Me too."

"Maybe they *will* develop a miracle cure."

Lucien shook his head. "Sometimes I think Delia's secretly happy that she got sick. That this is her way of getting back at Henry for cheating on her." When he'd initially called his mother by her first name, it had seemed mature and modern—but now, referring to *both* of his parents by name, *when they weren't present*, made him sound cool and detached like a psychiatrist. But who could blame him? "He was going to leave her, but then she got sick," Lucien added. "You knew that, didn't you?"

"I guess so," I lied.

"Janine says Delia is a very angry woman. I didn't believe her at first, but now I can see that she's right," Lucien confided. "My mother is one of those people who has always had unrealistic expectations. She really believed she was going to be the next Michelangelo . . . I hope your father realizes that she's *never* going to choose a headstone. *No* epitaph is *ever* going to be good enough for her."

"Papa will convince her to buy *something*," I answered. "He always does."

"We'll see," said Lucien—less invested than I was. "Say, do you want to go for a swim?"

"I don't have a bathing suit."

"You don't need one. I'm blind, remember? What am I going to see?"

"But your neighbors . . . ?

"Trust me, nobody is paying attention," said Lucien.

So I removed the pleated jade skirt, and the collared cotton blouse, and the prickly nylon tights, and folded them neatly on the chaise-longue. Then I dove into the water, wearing only my underwear, as unlike a Girl Scout as anyone has ever been.

. . . . .

I was overjoyed to learn that we would be returning to Scarsdale for a third time the following Saturday, that Delia Braithwaite hadn't been able—or willing—to choose a stone. My mother, needless to say, was far less pleased. When my father first told her, she stormed out into the carving yard, gathered up his favorite set of chisels, and dumped as many implements as she could carry into the murky stew of the nearby duck pond. She'd have done the same with his treasured stencils—a far more expensive tantrum—if Papa hadn't grabbed her by the arm.

"Let go of me!" shouted Mama.

Papa did not let go. "You've got to calm down, Eileen. I'll go phone Delia and tell her we're not coming back, and that will be the end of this."

"You'll do no such thing!"

"Be reasonable. She's expecting us. It's one thing to cancel on her, but I can't just not show up without telling her . . ."

"We're *not* cancelling," snapped Mama. "I'm going over there *with you*."

She wrested her arm from Papa's grasp and glared at him defiantly.

"That's fine by me," answered Papa—although I could tell that it wasn't. "Now please get a grip on yourself. You're out of control."

"I have every right to be out of control if I want to be," said my mother. "Most women would be out of control *under the circumstances*."

"Good God! There are no circumstances, Eileen. You know that."

"Don't get me upset," answered Mama. "I'm getting into bed, Gordon, and I don't want to hear another word about that woman. *Period*."

Papa spent the remainder of the evening recovering his missing equipment, wading into the stagnant water in his fishing boots and retrieving the chisels one by one. By midnight—when he finally gave up for the day—he'd recovered eight out of nine. Any sane person would have quit at that point, willing to swallow the loss of a ten dollar carving tool. But Papa kept at it for the next six evenings, leaving the dinner table before dessert and working into the early hours of the morning. Several nights he dragged me with him to hold the flashlight. Once, he even recruited Katie's hoodlum boyfriend to help him sweep the area with a heavy-duty net. Nothing. On the final night of our futile search, Papa explained his determination. "That was your grandfather's chisel," he told me. "I was a hoping it would be *your* chisel someday."

My first reaction was surprise—then anger. How could he possibly have thought that I wanted to sell tombstones for a living? The only constraint that kept me from setting that hideous Girl Scout uniform on fire immediately was the fear that he wouldn't let me accompany him to visit Delia and Lucien. Never had it crossed my mind that I would stay in the monument business any longer than Annie or Katie. But as soon as Papa planted the idea in my head, the path toward running the monument shop became increasingly clear. That was the obvious trajectory of my future life—not a life of ease and luxury in Lucien's strong arms. My father had been planning for the shop to stay in the family all along, much as he'd anticipated how Mama would ultimately handle her encounter with Delia. That explained the relaxed smile on his face the next Saturday as he prepared for our next drive up to Westchester.

"I'll bring the car around, Eileen," he said casually, twirling his keys around his thumb. "Can you please help Natalie with the sample cases?"

"I'm not going," Mama announced. Her voice was lethal with venom. "I don't owe it to that odious woman to take time out of my busy day to sell her a headstone. But let me make this clear, Gordon Luftig. This is the *last* time that you're going over there. *The last!* If you go over again, you'll come home to an empty house."

.....

When Delia Braithwaite greeted us that third Saturday, she made no pretense of wanting me to accompany my father and her into the parlor. "Be a dear, Natasha," she said, "and go keep Lucien company. He's upstairs, somewhere. You'll find him." At that moment, I swear I could have fallen to my knees and kissed the woman's slippers. I still despised her—for calling me by the wrong name, for flirting with Papa—but I was grateful nonetheless. I glanced quickly toward my father for permission, and then abandoned the pair of them in the entryway

The upstairs foyer was as elegant as its downstairs counterpart, but less coherent. The walls were lined with African tribal masks, and framed eighteenth century maps, and two massive surrealist canvases signed *Joan Miró*. Several free-standing nudes, clearly more Delia Braithwaite originals, cuddled in various corners. I heard music drifting from the far end of the hallway—Van Morrison's "Brown Eyed Girl"—and I followed it to a closed door. I drew the deepest breath that I've ever taken. Then I knocked.

"Come in!"

I opened the door. The room was three times the size of my own bedroom, a giant rectangle cluttered with ski equipment and free weights. A state-of-the-art sound system covered nearly an entire wall, while a second housed honeycombs of CDs. Lucien lay sprawled out on his queen-sized bed, shirtless, his arms splayed and his knees drawn up.

"It's Natalie," I said.

"I know," answered Lucien. "Same shampoo."

I crossed the room rapidly and sat down at the foot of the bed. This would be my last chance to spend time with Lucien, I realized—unless I did something drastic. And that was *exactly* what I intended to do. I knew deep down that I didn't have half a prayer of winning over a handsome high school senior with a college girlfriend—one who believed that I was an eleven- year-old Girl Scout—but I was going do my damnedest to try. I inched my way along the mattress until my hip was nearly touching Lucien's ear.

"I like you," I said—trying to keep my voice as steady as possible.

"Okay," said Lucien. "I like you too."

"I mean I like you *like a boyfriend*," I said.

I'd done it. I'd set myself up for Lucien to reject me, for yet another confirmation that I was thoroughly unlovable. Instead—to my amazement—my teenage dreamboat reached his arm across my waist, drawing my chest to his head. Seconds later, his lips were pressed to mine and his fingers were fumbling with the buttons of my uniform vest. Nothing in my romance novels had prepared me for the tingle of flesh upon flesh, the pleasure of Lucien's body braced gently above mine. That was when I started to hate him.

Maybe it was because he already had a girlfriend in Colorado—because he was cheating on her, just as Henry had cheated on

Delia. Maybe it was because he thought I was only eleven and not caring. Or maybe Lucien's greatest sin was being blind—liking me for who I was, rather than finding me physically alluring

So I let him finish. I let him do whatever he wanted, making no effort to stop him. And when he was done, I squeezed back into the jade skirt and collared cotton shirt, leaving the nylon tights bundled in a ball on the bedspread.

"Where are you going?" demanded Lucien.

I didn't answer. I slipped into the hallway, indifferent, letting him pepper the empty gray room with his questions.

On the way down to the white parlor, I took the stairs two at a time. My trefoil pin fell off and clattered against the landing, but I made no effort to recover it. I'd already decided that this was the last time that I would ever wear a Girl Scout uniform. If my father was going to stick to his business model, he was going to have to find another accomplice. I was *never* going to sell tombstones door-to-door again! I might have told my father as much in front of Delia, if her shouting hadn't stopped me short.

"What do you want me to say, Gordon? I was wrong," declared our hostess. "It has taken me thirty years to admit it to myself, but that doesn't make it any less true. If I'd found a way to keep you in Copenhagen, my life wouldn't be such a mess. Everything since then has been *a waste*. Except Lucien. I do love Lucien. But all the rest has been *a colossal waste*."

"You don't mean that," answered my father. "Any of that."

I tiptoed toward the parlor, pausing just before the open door. I could see the pair of them reflected in mirrored windows of the Louis XV armoire. They sat side-by-side on the sofa, Delia clutching my father's hairy forearm with both hands.

"You feel the same way, Gordon," said Delia. "There's no point in lying about it. I know you do. Why else would you drive out here *again and again*?"

"To sell you a headstone," said my father.

He did not sound like a man who believed what he was saying. When Delia started sobbing, he wrapped his arm around her shoulder and let her cry.

"It's okay," he said softly. "It's all going to be okay."

Delia broke away from his embrace."Bullshit. It's not going to be okay. . . . And you know you feel the same way I do, Gordon. You're just afraid to admit it. Like hell, you're trying to sell me a headstone. That daughter of yours isn't even a Girl Scout."

"I realize you're upset, but—"

"Don't lie to me, Gordon. She's not a Scout. Scouts don't salute with their left hands."

Papa nodded. "Natalie is not a Girl Scout," he conceded.

"You're in love with me, Gordon. I know you are!" Delia's voice was desperate now, devoid of any vestige of control. "Stop lying to yourself—lying to *everyone*—and at least have the decency to admit that I'm right. You're still in love with me . . . and I am going to die."

Delia Braithwaite's voice choked up as she acknowledged her impending mortality, and Papa waited patiently for all the tears to drain out of her. He didn't say another word until she'd dried her eyes on a tissue and stanched her streaming makeup.

"So?" she asked. "I trust you, Gordon. I think you might be the only person left in the world who I really trust. So please tell me. What should I do now?"

Papa took her hand in his and leaned forward, as though he might kiss her. His entire body was trembling, and he wore an expression of suppressed pain—as though he'd stepped on a nail but was unwilling to scream. "I think you should talk this over with your husband," he said softly. "Our best package is a 'his-and-hers' special. You place both epitaphs on one long stone when the first spouse passes, and then later all you do is carve in the surviving partner's dates." My father's tone shifted slowly from intimate, to *false* intimate—the voice he used to clinch the bargain with his other customers. "It's the best way to go about matters, particularly if you have children. Everything is taking care of in advance. Far less strain on them." Papa patted the back of Delia Braithwaite's hand. "It's the arrangement I have with my own wife," he added, a reassuring smile taking hold of his lips. "Honestly, it's the most reasonable deal around."

Ad Valorem

George had handled their taxes. All year long, he tucked receipts and invoices into a battle-scarred manila envelope with a string-tie seal that he kept in his lower desk drawer alongside the church-warden pipes he hadn't smoked in two decades and the July 1958 copy of *Playboy* that he'd shoplifted as a teenager. During early March, as the first crocuses poked their pastel heads through the fractured earth behind the kitchen, Greta's husband drove to Creve Coeur, Rhode Island, where a CPA named Felix Ingersoll—a solo practitioner she'd never met—completed and filed the returns for a modest fee. They'd discovered Ingersoll in the yellow pages, when they'd first opened the printing shop and their finances had grown complicated. Even after they'd relocated to New London, only ten minute's walk from a tidy, brick-and-mortar H&R block office, George continued to rely upon their "no frills" storefront accountant. The man still employed the same desktop calculator he'd used at their first meeting; he advanced their estimated taxes from his own escrow account and let them reimburse him at their convenience—not because he was particularly trusting, he assured George, but because his late father, who'd run "the firm" before him, had always done it that way. Yet at times, when the printing shop's cash flow backed up, this amounted to a short-term, no interest business loan, for which they were exceedingly grateful. Photocopied receipts dating back thirty years lined the entire upper shelf of their pantry, bound neatly with rubber bands, in preparation for an eventual audit. But Ingersoll had a nephew at the local I.R.S. field office, so that day never arrived. And now George's ashes had been sprinkled over Narragansett Bay, irrevocably beyond the government's reach.

Greta had started saving the receipts herself on the morning after his first stroke, knowing he'd want them when he recovered. She'd made no effort to distinguish business expenses from personal expenses, shipments of industrial-strength toner from parking fees at Memorial Hospital. George would sort that all out. But then the second hemorrhage followed the first, like an earthquake succeeding a tremor, and she found herself stuffing canary-colored forms labeled CASKET and HEADSTONE, GRANITE into George's trusty envelope. She amassed the receipts mechanically, much as she replaced the burnt-out sodium bulbs in the porch lights and phoned the lawn care company to shut off the sprinkler pipes for the winter—taking stock, each day, of the many things that her husband had done and would no longer do. So when an early warm spell hit, and the first purple crocus braved the residue of patchy snow, Greta phoned Ingersoll to arrange for an appointment. The accountant sounded friendlier on the phone than she'd anticipated, far less musty, his voice deep and resonant like a seasoned cello. But the man hadn't asked after George. He'd merely inquired what day of the week she preferred to come in, as though her calling was nothing out of the ordinary. Maybe he feared that she and George had separated, and he was trying to be polite. Or maybe he just didn't care. In any case, here she was in Creve Coeur with a year's collection of fading receipts.

The morning was bright and breezy, the bracing air off the harbor weighed down with salt and mist and memories of fishing excursions with her long-deceased in-laws. Those had been in the late 1970s—a generation ago—when Creve Coeur still supplied an entire continent with outboard motors, electric sewing machines, costume jewelry. What remained of the jewelry trade had since shifted to the suburbs, abandoning the narrow downtown alleyways to pawn shops and fast-food outlets. Ingersoll's office, just off Oxbow Street on the less-fashionable slope of Banker's Hill, now sat sandwiched between an Eritrean Cultural Center and the Best-Way Driving Academy. Farther up the sidewalk, at the entrance to the landmark Balk & Twimble Building, a turbaned Sikh sold croissants and soups to a trickle of office workers. In the accountant's window, a solitary gray blind hung behind the pane where "L. Ingersoll & Son" formed a faded gilt arc. Greta opened the accountant's door and stepped into the cluttered office. Inside, the air smelled faintly of varnish. A pair of face-to-face tanker desks, and the formidable row of identical steel filing cabinets, instantly reminded her of the urban police stations depicted on Nixon-era television shows. The accountant reclined at one of the desks, eyes closed, arms tucked behind his balding head, listening to an Oldies station on a portable radio: The Drifters. *Save the Last Dance for Me.* He looked up when Greta entered and quickly shut off the music. Then he adjusted his tie.

Two Hummel figurines stood on his desk: A bookkeeper with a pencil over one ear, and an officious-looking nurse. Also a marble bust of Beethoven. A bumper-sticker plastered against the nearest filing cabinet warned: *There are only three types of accountants. Those who can count and those who can't.* Greta had to read the message several times before she understood that this wasn't a genuine error.

"Mrs. Starling?" asked Ingersoll. He steered her toward a red leather swivel chair that oozed synthetic stuffing through a wound along its flank. "I don't think we've had the pleasure of meeting before, have we?"

Greta seated herself on the crippled chair. It sagged under her weight. She laid the manila envelope atop Ingersoll's desk blotter.

"My husband handled the taxes," she said. But the words, as soon as she heard them, sounded too cold, so she added, "George raved about the laughs you two had together. He swore you were a regular Jack Benny—not that he ever remembered the punch lines to your jokes."

Ingersoll leaned toward her, his orbicular eyes gleaming. "How many CPAs does it take to change a light bulb?"

Greta smiled politely. "How many?"

"It depends. How much money do you have?"

The accountant grinned—and after a short, distinct pause—he let forth a rich belly laugh that rattled his entire body. Unexpectedly, Greta found herself laughing along with him, although the joke wasn't terribly funny. It was the first time that she had laughed in many months. When she tried to stop laughing, she found herself seized with a second paroxysm of hysterics, and she bit into her lower lip to keep quiet. Ingersoll had already opened her envelope and skimmed the contents.

"How *is* George?" he asked. "Well, I hope."

His tone suggested that he foresaw George wasn't well.

"George passed on," said Greta, clutching the purse in her lap. "He had a stroke in October."

Ingersoll nodded. He toyed with the buttons on his jacket sleeve. In the corner, a dehumidifier droned indifferently. "My Betty too," said the accountant. "December. Cancer of the pancreas."

He retrieved a framed photo from a desk drawer: a cheerful, iron-haired matron posing at the base of the Jefferson Memorial. Betty Ingersoll stood arms akimbo, framed by the reflection of cherry blossoms on the Potomac. Greta returned the photograph to the widower and inspected him more closely—as though their similar misfortunes had earned him her notice. Ingersoll certainly cut a distinguished figure, despite the wisps of dark hair protruding from his immense ears; he was probably closer to seventy than sixty. What struck Greta most was the unmistakable sadness that the man wore around his deep-set eyes and the corners of his mouth. The sadness was almost painted on, like a clown's, as though every smile demanded agonizing exertion. She couldn't help wonder if she also bore such visible marks of grief.

"Death and taxes," said Ingersoll. He examined the Beethoven bust reflectively, shifting it from one large hand to the other. "In the long run, you can't cheat either one."

"Though with taxes," answered Greta, "you can certainly give it a shot."

What had inspired her to say such a peculiar thing? This wasn't at all how she felt about tax-paying. Some of the other business owners in the Chamber of Commerce did hold rather parochial—even retrograde—views on politics, but she and George had always prided themselves on their liberalism and civic virtue. Now she was ashamed to have this stranger believing she felt otherwise.

"I'll do the best I can for you, Mrs. Starling. Within limits," said Ingersoll. "I'm truly sorry about your husband."

The accountant rose—with some effort—and extended his firm hand, clasping hers between his palms. For the first time, Greta took note of the Styrofoam dinner boxes overflowing the wastepaper basket. She had also been surviving on carry-out meals for months, ever since her daughter had returned to California. Ellen had responsibilities of her own, of course. Cats. A restaurant to manage. It couldn't be helped.

"I'm sorry too," said Greta. "About your wife, I mean."

"Forty-two years." Ingersoll grimaced. "That's a long time."

Greta was already at the door, when the strangest notion popped into her head. "Didn't you tell something to George last year? Something odd. About lettuce and emperors?"

"Lettuce... emperors?" echoed Ingersoll. "Oh. I suppose I told him about Diocletian, the Roman Emperor, who retired to the Adriatic coast to raise cabbages.... Last spring, I was thinking of retiring to my garden. That was before Betty's diagnosis."

"Of course," said Greta. "Diocletian. Cabbages."

She stepped out into the brisk New England afternoon. Her parking meter hadn't expired and the line had evaporated at the lunch cart. When she telephoned the printing shop, the part-time college girl at the counter assured her that everything was in order. So this would be just another routine, uneventful day without her husband.

Greta treated herself to a Bavarian cream donut and wiped her eyes with the complimentary napkin. Afterwards, she filled up her gas tank and drove back to Connecticut.

And that was that.

.....

Only that wasn't that.

Greta's bedtime had been creeping earlier all winter, so that now she barely kept her eyes open past twilight. Without George's company, what was the point? Besides, she told herself, waking at dawn and sleeping at dusk was nature's plan. But this new schedule meant that frequently she dozed off with the overhead lights still illuminated, and those evenings, she often suffered through the wildest nightmares. On the night after her visit to Ingersoll, Greta dreamed that the I.R.S. had repossessed her husband—and that she could only recover him if she paid off the back taxes. In the dream, she had the tenacity of Scarlet O'Hara trying to save her plantation. When she woke up, lacquered in a sheen of perspiration, her first thought was to share the dream with George.

Later that night, too drained for more sleep, she sat on a stepstool in the walk-in closet and folded George's slacks and jackets into a cardboard box for Goodwill. Her husband's lush scent still clung to the wool—a distinctive aroma halfway between aftershave and raw leather—and in the breast pocket of his seersucker blazer, she found an index card with a list of unusual vanity license plates that he'd seen around town: GONLOCO, KVECH 22, IH8PL8S. That was *so* George! To be amused by the minor foibles of his neighbors, to collect something of absolutely no tangible value. He had an entire shoebox full of these cards, each blanketed front-and-back with amusing alpha-numeric combinations—like Egyptian tablets coated with hieroglyphics. Greta thought about these cards, and somehow they reminded her of Ingersoll. How lonely the accountant had seemed. How forlorn! Contented people might share funny stories, but only injured souls told canned jokes with such frequency. Greta pictured Ingersoll sitting alone in that dimly-lit, under-trafficked office, clinging to his few remaining clients, while in the background WTXB counted down the greatest romantic hits of 1963. A sixth sense told her that Ingersoll didn't have children, that he and Betty had been a team of only two. Yet the accountant had seemed such a gentlemanly old soul. The sort of man—like George—who lacked pretense, who valued integrity for its own sake. Felix Ingersoll would have made a fine father, thought Greta. He would have spoiled a daughter with summer camps in the Berkshires and spring breaks on the Gulf Coast—just as George had indulged Ellen—and the girl, if she'd existed, would have adored him.

The next morning, Greta left the printing shop under the authority of the part-time college girl, Valerie—or was it Vanessa?—and drove across town to the municipal library. She was no stranger to making use of the library, but only as a poor woman's bookstore, feeding herself a bland-but-pleasing diet of two bestselling mystery novels each week. George, whose tastes had run more literary, was always encouraging her to read the classics, but with a mischievous gleam in his eyes, because he knew that she never would. Today, Greta sneaked a cup of decaf into the reference room and commandeered a secluded carrel. For the better part of the day, she immersed herself in ancient history: Martindale's *The Prosopography of the Later Roman Empire*, Chastagnol's *From the Severan Dynasty to the Tetrarchy.* By the time the shouts of schoolchildren announced the start of their four o'clock story hour, she knew more about the Emperor Diocletian than she did about any living human being. Some of the texts ran miles above her head—she had to look up the definition of prosopography—but she found her historical investigation to be quite comforting. *Irrationally so.* Because, in some subtle yet cosmic way, it brought her closer to the sad-faced accountant.

Greta checked out as many books as she could carry. Not only sources on Diocletian, but a hefty biography of Constantine and the first three volumes of Gibbon's *Decline and Fall of the Roman Empire*. Also *Classics for Dummies*. On a whim, she called her daughter from the payphone at the Greek pizzeria opposite the Veterans of Foreign Wars post. It was three hours earlier in San Francisco, the height of the lunch service at Ellen's upscale bistro.

"Can you hear me, honey?" asked Greta. "I'm calling from a payphone."

"Get a cell phone, Mom. *Please*," said Ellen. Then: "I can hear you just fine."

Greta raised her voice anyway. "What would you say if I went back to graduate school and got a degree in ancient history?"

"Sure, Mom. If that's what you want."

"I was reading about the crisis of the third century," continued Greta. "About the defeat of Carinus and the intrigues of Constantius Chlorus. To tell you the truth, honey, until today I'd never even heard of Constantius Chlorus."

"Can we talk about this tonight, Mom? I'm at work."

In the background, Greta heard shouting about anchovies. She couldn't imagine how she'd become less important than anchovies!

"What would you say if I decided to get remarried?" asked Greta.

"I'd be very happy for you," said Ellen. "I've got to go."

That was not the answer Greta had wanted. It was intolerably reasonable.

"I love you," said Ellen. "I'll call you later."

And then Greta was listening to a dial tone. She held the receiver to her ear until a prerecorded operator warned her to hang up and dial again if she wanted to make a call.

.....

Whatever glow remained from her ad-hoc historical research wore off after supper. Greta sat at the kitchen table, drawing circles in her chow-mein with her chopsticks. She considered phoning a friend—her sister-in-law; one of the widows from her bereavement circle—but there wasn't anyone she particularly wanted to speak to. When Ellen called her, she hovered over the answering machine while the girl left a lengthy, apologetic message. Later, reading *Classics for Dummies* in bed, Greta folded shut the book halfway through the Battle of Salamis and dashed barefoot into George's study. She felt inside his humidor, emptied out the gourmet cookie tin where he'd kept his military discharge papers, rummaged through drawers full of hand-carved chess pieces, and obsolete national park brochures, and a set of ophthalmoscope heads that he'd inherited from his great uncle. What she was looking for, she finally unearthed, crumpled and coffee-stained, behind a dieffenbachia plant, where it had most likely missed the wastepaper basket. A receipt! It was for a two pound sack of bird seed, but it was a receipt none-the-less. Later, she discovered a substantially larger receipt for the tuxedo rental from the marriage of their neighbors' son. That was good enough, she decided. So what if she made a fool of herself?! Even the risk of humiliation was better than roaming an empty house, weeping, until someone found her dead.

Greta slept fitfully that night and hit the road at sun-up. It was Holy Thursday. The radio news reported ad nauseam on the Bishop of Connecticut's early morning homily and the reenacted cleansing of the apostles' feet. If she'd been religious, losing George might have been more tolerable—maybe—if she'd been able to console herself with the promise of reunion in an afterlife of harps and halos. But deep down, Greta knew that you had only your time on earth, nothing more, and as fleeting as her years with George suddenly seemed, she had no reason to expect any others. She arrived in Creve Coeur just as the bells of St. Catherine's announced late mass to Episcopalians and told non-believers that it was time to feed their parking meters.

The Sikh was already manning his post in front of the Balk & Twimble building, but the accountant's door was still locked. Greta purchased a copy of the *Providence Journal* and dried the dew off a park bench in a nearby traffic island. She browsed the news without focus, glancing across the avenue every few seconds to take a peek at the entryway to Ingersoll's office. Shortly after ten o'clock, fearing he'd managed to slip past her, she re-checked the door. But the accountant wasn't there yet... and he didn't appear by eleven fifteen... or noon. Why should he be there, really? For all Greta knew, Thursdays were Ingersoll's day off. Or he might have cleared his schedule that morning to pay a visit to his dead wife at the cemetery. Whatever the poor man's reasons, she'd been crazy to assume that he'd be at his office, waiting for her, as though he had nothing better to do. *As though he owed her something!*

Greta found a blank postcard in her purse—creased, but serviceable. The card was an extra, left over from their holiday in England two years earlier; the face depicted Stonehenge at winter solstice. Now, Greta pressed out the folds as best as she could and scrawled a brief note to the accountant. Nothing personal, certainly nothing too forward—just a polite request to incorporate these additional receipts into her returns. Then she clipped the papers together and slid them under the office door, giving the final corner of the card an extra push for good measure.

She ambled back toward the parking lot, beset with a sudden emptiness. For the first time, she wondered why George—who kept such meticulous records—had discarded the birdseed receipt. Yet another of those minor mysteries it was too late to solve, like precisely where her ancestors had come from in Germany, or what she would have been named if she'd been born a boy. Only when she returned to her car did Greta recognize how foolish she had been to stuff the receipts under the door. Without them, she would have no pretext for returning to Creve Coeur. She charged back around the corner, her heels wobbling, trying to conjure up a way to retrieve her note.

Felix Ingersoll was standing at his open door. He rested one hand on the knob and held her postcard in the other.

"Oh," said Greta, startled. "You're here."

"Mrs. Starling," said Ingersoll.

"I was just . . ." said Greta.

She couldn't think of an explanation, so she fell mute.

"You could have mailed these," said the accountant. "I won't get around to your returns for at least several weeks."

"I didn't want to take any chances," answered Greta.

"But such a long drive," said Ingersoll. The accountant smiled at her, holding her gaze for a moment longer than necessary—maybe a hint that he too was becoming aware of her as more than a client. He looked as though he might ask her an intimate question, possibly even invite her out for lunch. Or, more likely, it was all her fancy. When he finally did speak, he said: "I think I can get you a better deal on your taxes." Yet even his own words seemed to surprise him, as though he'd offered her an unplanned gift. "Because of your changed circumstances," he added. "I know it's not exactly a silver lining, but it is *something*."

"Thank you," she said. "I'd appreciate that."

Greta repeated this phrase to herself on the long drive back to New London. *I'd appreciate that. I'd appreciate that.* Over and over again, she echoed the decisive words. Like a parakeet gone haywire. She could not imagine any surer or stupider way to end a conversation.

.....

That night Greta hated herself. She should have taken better care of her body while George was alive: looked after her figure, moisturized. Maybe even shelled out for those anti-wrinkle injections in her forehead. Because what sort of man was going to fall for a plump fifty-eight-year-old widow with swollen ankles and crow's feet? Certainly not a handsome, financially-independent widower like Felix Ingersoll. Men like that wanted smooth skin and taut midriffs, at least the second time around. All she had to offer was heartfelt affection—and, as of that week, a conversational, if sporadic, knowledge of later antiquity. Which meant she might well live another forty years, sleeping alone in this draughty oversized house, toxic memories haunting the mirrors, and the bed sheets cold as death beside her.

All that kept her going at the printing shop the next day was the hope that Ingersoll might phone—that he would finally muster the courage to ask what he hadn't dared outside the door of his office. But Greta returned home that night to find only two blinking messages on the answering machine, one from her daughter and the other to remind George that his high school reunion was approaching.

Maybe he's playing it cool, Greta told herself. Waiting three days, trying not to appear over-anxious. Not that she wanted a man who played games at Ingersoll's age, but she'd make do. Besides, it would be romantic—in an endearing way—if he actually cared *that* much.

Three days passed. Saturday. Sunday. Monday. *Nothing.*

A terrible darkness settled over her—a crushing misery worse that she'd even felt in the long days after she'd lost George. Greta drugged herself to sleep on her husband's leftover back medication. If she'd been a brave woman—a less conventional woman—she might have consumed the whole bottle. But when she thought of what this would do to Ellen, she grew nauseous, so she limited herself to three azure pills.

Ingersoll's call finally came on Tuesday morning, just as Greta was stepping out of the shower. She nearly fell down the stairs, racing for the telephone.

"Mrs. Starling?" said Ingersoll. "It's Felix Ingersoll. The accountant."

"Goodness. What a surprise," answered Greta.

A wave of joy swept through her. Hearing his rich voice was all that it took.

"I'm not disturbing you, am I? I'm not calling too early."

"Not at all," said Greta.

She was wearing only a bath towel. Speaking to the accountant while water trickled down her bare shoulders made her feel sexier than she had in years. Anyone passing by the house might see her half-naked body through the sheer kitchen drapes, but even that didn't bother her. What did she have to be ashamed of?

"You're missing June," said Ingersoll.

"Excuse me?"

"Not all of it. Only a few weeks, early in the month," he continued. "With anyone else, I probably wouldn't have said anything. But you've always been so scrupulous . . ."

"Are you sure you can't find them?"

She heard the irritation in her voice. How dare he call her *on business*, about a couple of missing receipts? Who the hell did he think he was?

"Maybe I'm overlooking something obvious," said Ingersoll. "Honestly, I've been known to do that before."

It was hard to imagine Felix Ingersoll overlooking anything. At the same time, it was also difficult to imagine George misplacing two weeks' worth of receipts. Greta groped through the recesses of her addled brain: Where had the two of them been in early June? Home in New London, as far as she could recall. Working; gardening. Playing contract bridge with Mort and Mandy Ballister on Wednesdays. Burning through hours as though they would live forever.

"It's not a big deal, really," said Ingersoll. "I just thought—"

"I was planning to be in Creve Coeur later this afternoon," said Greta. "Why don't I stop by and take a look?"

"All right. Why not?" he answered—an undertone of nerves seeping into his usually steady voice. "It might be helpful. If it's not too inconvenient, that is."

So he *wanted* her to come, she thought. She could hear her pulse in her ears.

After she said goodbye to the accountant—with a one o'clock "appointment" in her pocket—she immediately called Ellen. It was five a.m. in California. Greta realized this *after* she'd already punched her daughter's number into the phone.

"What's wrong?" the girl demanded. "You're not sick, are you?"

"I'm sorry it's so early," said Greta. "I just spoke to the accountant. Mr. Ingersoll. You remember Daddy talking about Mr. Ingersoll, don't you?"

"It's five in the morning, Mom. It's *dark* out."

"He thinks he can get me a better deal on the taxes. Because Daddy died, you know. I realize it's not a silver lining, but it *is* something."

Greta heard a groan in the background. It sounded like a man, not a cat.

"I thought your taxes went *up* when you were single," said Ellen. "Anyway, we really can't talk about this right now. You're not going senile, Mom, are you? Please tell me you're not losing it..."

"I'm fine, honey," said Greta. "I just wanted to share the good news."

.....

Five hours later, Greta once again found herself crossing the threshold of Felix Ingersoll's accounting office. She instantly noticed the changes since her earlier visit: gone were the overflowing wastepaper basket, the stacks of yellowing newspapers, the multiple wire-mesh trays full of typewriter ribbons and assorted rubber bands. Everything now appeared tidy, organized. The evergreen scent of cleanser had replaced the odor of varnish. Even the solitary gray blind had been elevated to shoulder-level, letting sunlight bathe the front two-thirds of the room. Ingersoll reclined at his desk as though nothing was amiss, but he sported a stylish tweed jacket over an equally snazzy silk shirt. A burgundy handkerchief protruded from his breast pocket. Greta wouldn't let herself believe that he'd done all of this *for her*.

The Oldies station was still playing on the portable radio. *Earth Angel*. The Penguins. Ingersoll didn't shut it off.

"I did some spring cleaning," he said. "It was about time."

Greta seated herself on the damaged leather chair without being asked. "I know what you mean. I still can't bring myself to empty out George's study," she said. But then she regretted bringing up George. "It looks nice," she added. "Very nice."

Ingersoll beamed. "What is the definition of an accountant?"

"I give up. What?"

"Someone who solves a problem you did not know you had," he answered, "in a way you don't understand."

Ingersoll chuckled. Greta laughed too.

"That's not such a bad thing, sometimes," said Greta. "When someone solves a problem you didn't know you had."

The last bars of *Earth Angel* drifted into silence—and then into an advertisement for anti-baldness medication. Ingersoll snapped off the radio. "I *like* being bald," he said. "What I disliked was throwing away money on barbers."

Greta wasn't accustomed to this breed of surly humor, but she enjoyed it. She couldn't help thinking how different this lonely man was from George. Not better or worse, just *different*. George's jokes—the few he ever told—had been more like amusing anecdotes, slice-of-life vignettes of the *Readers' Digest* variety. At the same time, she also detected an underlying wariness in Ingersoll—nothing pernicious, but more like a healthy sense of suspicion. Maybe this is what came of preparing other people's taxes. She couldn't imagine George—*if he had been the survivor*—cleaning out the printing shop on three days' notice to impress a widowed Betty Ingersoll.

"I've been reading up on Diocletian," said Greta—apropos of virtually nothing. "It's frightful how little history I know."

Ingersoll gazed at her without answering. She feared she'd said something humiliating, and she felt her cheeks burning. But then she realized that the accountant hadn't heard her. That he hadn't been listening at all.

"Would you like to go for a walk, Mrs. Starling?" he asked suddenly—a bit too formally, almost stilted, as though he'd been practicing the question for weeks. "It's such a fine day . . . and it *is* the first day of spring."

If he hadn't told her, she never would have known.

"You wouldn't mind, would you? When we get back, we'll find your receipts."

"I'd be delighted," answered Greta. "Truly."

So that's how it began. Easily, almost too easily. He led her through the once-classy Yankee neighborhoods, pointed out the churchyard where Louisa May Alcott's sisters were buried and the Victorian porch from which the Red Ribbon Stranger had kidnapped the Stanton girl. Greta had been born in Creve Coeur—she'd lived there for the first twenty-eight years of her life—but, in her youth, she'd never really thought about what had come before her. In contrast, Ingersoll knew what year each block of the city had been laid out and which Presidential candidate had given which speech off which balcony; he also joked that he knew the approximate tax assessments of all the homes they passed, though he promised not to bore her with the figures. Somehow, all this knowledge increased Greta's sympathy for Ingersoll. Only a man without children could invest so much energy in his neighbors' finances, and their architectural idiosyncrasies, and the laying-in dates of their cornerstones. Somehow, she started calling him Felix, and then she had her hand on his elbow. They stood side by side at the waterfront, looking out over the railing, in a grassy enclave between loading docks.

Angry smoke rose from the refinery across the harbor. Gulls circled above the canopy of barges and tankers that nearly obscured the underlying water.

"Do you want to hear something funny?" Ingersoll asked.

"Another one of your bookkeeping jokes?"

"A poem," answered Ingersoll. "It's a Felix Ingersoll original. I call it *The Accountant*."

He thrust his chest out and declaimed:

He was a very cautious man, who never romped or played.
He never smoked, he never drank, nor even kissed a maid.
And when he up and passed away, insurance was denied.
For since he hadn't ever lived, they claimed he never died.

Greta understood that he was trying to be funny, but she dug her fingernails into the base of her thumb to keep from giggling. Somehow, seeing this older man holding forth with such vigor, she feared that laughter might offend him—particularly because she had encountered this "Felix Ingersoll original" before, on a dinner program she'd printed for the retirement roast of a local rabbi. The accountant's performance reminded Greta of the occasion when Ellen had memorized an Edmund Burke oration for a sixth grade speech contest—and instead of calling society a "fierce organism," she'd mistakenly referred to it, *in front of the entire junior high school*, as a "fierce orgasm." Greta's smirk gave way to an unintended guffaw, and she squeezed Ingersoll's forearm.

"They don't call me the Robert Frost of loopholes for nothing," said Ingersoll.

Greta tugged his lapels so that he was facing her. He stood a full head taller than she was, just the height to kiss him on tiptoes.

"I'm not short any receipts, am I?" she asked.

"Betty and I owned a boat," he answered. "It's docked down at the Watch Hill Marina. If you'd like, we could take it out next weekend and explore the bay."

"You're avoiding the question," said Greta. "I drove all the way down here because my June receipts were missing—but I don't think they are. I think you lied through your teeth in order to invite me on a walk."

Ingersoll shrugged. "You'll forgive me?"

"Quite possibly," she said. "I'll tell you on the boat ride."

He didn't kiss her, after that. He escorted her back to her car and hugged her tentatively, then waved as she pulled out into traffic.

.....

She ought to have been happy, Greta told herself. She had a *right* to be happy. But just as she'd been unable to feel genuine sadness during the first weeks after she'd lost George, she now felt emotionally blocked—maybe the fine fabric of her heart was too tattered for joy. Or maybe it was survivor's guilt. In either case, every time she reflected on Ingersoll's invitation to join him on his boat, her mind skipped—like a scratched record—to recollections of her fishing jaunts with George and his parents. The older Starlings had died, one after another, within weeks of each other. "His-and-hers" aneurysms, just like matching monogrammed towels. Maybe that was the way it was supposed to be done: that the widow's only true solace was to climb stoically into her husband's funeral pyre. Why else did an outing with Felix Ingersoll feel both so appealing and so wrong? She'd stand in front of the bedroom mirror, trying on various blouses she might wear for the excursion, then suddenly she'd find herself immersed in memories of an Independence Day fishing jaunt, shortly after their marriage, when her cotton sunhat had blown into Narragansett Bay, and George, fully-clothed, had plunged into the water to rescue it. A voice in the back of Greta's head heard her late father-in-law, a retired civil engineer and intransigent Hoover Republican, warning: *If it seems too good to be true, it most certainly is false.* So it was in a spirit of increasing self-doubt, coupled with self-denial, that Greta latched onto her daughter's idle musing, *I thought your taxes went up when you were single . . .*

She sat down on the side of the double bed and scoured Ellen's words for hidden meaning, as though examining a rare Latin text, slowly convincing herself that Ingersoll might not be the white knight he had appeared. Wouldn't a man who'd lied so easily to lure her back to his office also play fast-and-loose with his business practices—particularly if he had no reason to fear scrutiny? She remembered how confidently he'd spoken to George of the nephew in the I.R.S. field office—and how grateful they'd been at the time. In contrast to Felix Ingersoll, simultaneously tortured and shielded by his perennial wariness, her own late husband had been a man both easily loved and easily cheated. And she'd known this all along, hadn't she? Like a devoted wife who had convinced herself of a philandering husband's fidelity, she'd suppressed hunches about the accountant from the outset. Now, Greta gathered up all of the summer attire that she'd blanketed across the bedspread—floral-print skirts that hardly still fit her, frivolous halter-tops that she might never wear again. What the occasion called for was a modest, no-nonsense outfit, she decided—as though dressing sensibly could make up for her earlier blindness. She held the frilly white chemise with the embroidered blue anchors against her chest one final time. But recalling George as he clambered over the railing of his father's pleasure boat, presenting that soaked sunhat to her like a prince offering a glass slipper, she understood what she must do. One way or another, she needed to know the truth about Felix Ingersoll.

The next morning, Greta climbed up onto the wooden stepstool in the pantry and retrieved the previous year's binder of photocopied receipts. George had taken great care to preserve the documents, as though he was looking after a friend's album of priceless stamps. That's how her husband had always been: forward-looking, painstaking. After he'd died, she'd discovered that even the perpetual care on his cemetery plot had been prepaid. All she'd had to do was sign the forms and gather the receipts. So when Greta lugged the heavy, overstuffed binder down the street to the H&R Block office, she knew that, for better or for worse, their every last credit and expenditure was thoroughly accounted for.

She had walked past this lowslung structure thousands of times, but she'd never before been inside. The lobby boasted a row of immaculately-tended purple tradescantia plants running along the window sill; only on closer inspection did Greta realize that the sleek, silky leaves were made of plastic. A rack of glossy brochures pitched a wide assortment of financial planning services and high-interest annuities, but the spry, graying couples in the photographs looked indistinguishable from the spry, graying couples who pitched cosmetic implants from brochures in her dentist's lobby. Greta filled out a one-page form attached to a clipboard, and waited nearly an hour.

The woman who finally assisted her—more of a girl, really, with thick-framed glasses and hair frizzled like hemp—didn't understand what she wanted, at least not initially. "So you still haven't filed a return for last year?" the girl asked. "You photocopied your receipts, but you didn't file a return?"

"I *did* file a return," Greta explained—for the third time. "What I'd like for you to do is to *recalculate* what I owe. The photocopies of the receipts are so you can figure out my business deductions."

The girl shot Greta a look of intense displeasure. "That's a special order," she snapped. "Same-day service doesn't apply to special orders."

"Could you have it done by Thursday?"

"Friday at noon," said the girl.

"Thursday would be much better," pleaded Greta. "If there's a surcharge of some sort, that's really not a problem."

The girl frowned indignantly, as though she'd been offered a bribe, and when she once again said, "Friday at noon," her words actually sounded like a threat.

"Okay, Friday at noon," agreed Greta. "I'll be here at twelve-oh-one."

. . . . .

Ingersoll phoned the following evening to confirm their weekend plans. He reminded her to bring along a sweater, because the open water could prove breezy. Again, she thought of George and her drenched sunhat.

"I should have your tax returns completed by then," Ingersoll added—sounding quite pleased with himself. "I've saved you far more than I ever anticipated. Compared to the last few years, you're practically making a profit."

"Am I really?" asked Greta.

"I'll bring them along for your signature," he offered, "if you're willing to mix business with pleasure."

"Whatever you want, Felix," she agreed. "I have complete faith in you."

The accountant phoned back an hour later, to ask if she had any dietary preferences for their voyage, but she didn't pick up. She allowed his multiple messages to accumulate as the weekend approached, relishing the sound of his voice on her answering machine, the vowels strong and opulent and as broad as the Kennedy's. At the same time, she found her feelings for him acutely painful, because she anticipated what she would learn from the H&R Block audit, long before she arrived at twelve o'clock sharp on Friday, and waited three hours for her personalized report.

Greta carried the sealed manila envelope to a park bench on Halliday Street, opposite a playground, and slid the pages out with trembling fingers. Then she sat there for nearly half an hour, without looking down, while the schoolchildren shouted joyfully on the teeter-totters and monkey bars. She remembered when Ellen had been that age—how the other children had wanted their mothers to push them on the swings and to admire their sandcastles, while her daughter had insisted on exploring the world on her own. If there had been a payphone nearby, she might have called California. But to say what? She was fifty-eight years old. She ought to be able to take care of herself.

When Greta finally mustered the courage to compare the totals on the computer-generated spreadsheet—what they had owed versus what they had actually paid—the figures weren't even close. Ingersoll had obviously pocketed the difference. How easily he must have sized George up as a model victim—trusting, noble-hearted George, who in thirty-two years of marriage hadn't doubled-checked a single plumbing invoice or a restaurant tab. And maybe the accountant really did have a nephew at the IRS, to cover for him if his clients ever grew suspicious. Who could know for sure? All that mattered was that her father-in-law had been right: Anything that seemed too good to be true would inevitably prove false. It never once crossed Greta's mind that Ingersoll's figures had been accurate and the error belonged to H&R Block. This was simply how matters stood, she told herself. As clear as the bold numerals at the bottom of her recalculated tax returns. But how deeply, desperately she had longed for it to be otherwise, even after she'd arranged for the retrospective audit. To the very last moment, she had wanted to hate herself for doubting the integrity of Felix Ingersoll.

Greta could forgive the accountant *almost* anything, she decided. At fifty-eight, she was willing to forgive *anyone* almost anything. But not only had Felix Ingersoll robbed her blind, he'd made a fool of the man she'd loved. How could she ever absolve him of *that*? She was seized with a sudden impulse to share her disillusionment with the frolicking children—to warn them that life was bound to disappoint. After returning the forms to their envelope, she gazed through the cast iron bars of the gate that enclosed the nearby playground, envious of the happy-go-lucky girls in pigtails. That such innocence could exist on the same planet as her own despair rendered her speechless. She was too heartbroken to scream and too enraged to sob.

On the drive to the coast, Greta listened to WTXB: *Rainy Days and Mondays*; the Everly Brothers covering *Bye-Bye Love*; Barbara Streisand and Neil Diamond crooning *You Don't Bring Me Flowers*. Each tragic song reminded her that she was soon to be the one sitting alone in a house as still as death, while the radio recycled the romantic torch songs of her childhood. At first, this merely saddened her, but soon the self-pity gave way to outright rage—all of it directed at the duplicitous accountant. By the time Greta finally arrived at the Watch Hill Marina, she had worked herself up into something of a frenzy. Ingersoll's boat was, rightfully speaking, *her* boat and *George's* boat and the boat of *God-knows-how-many other innocent sops* who had trusted this monstrous man to treat them squarely. Her emotions were no longer blocked. Now they were raw. A volatile fury struggled to overcome a lifetime of self-restraint.

The Watch Hill Marina was a private harbor that served several adjacent country clubs along the coast of Narragansett Bay.

The anchorage stood at the end of a quiet, winding road of sand dunes and pine barrens—a striking contrast to the noisy public jetty where her in-laws had once docked their motorboat. Greta followed the wooden signs toward the waterfront. She waited several minutes at an automated barrier while a bulky, uniformed officer phoned ahead to announce her arrival. This delay had not been part of Greta's plan. She had wanted to surprise the accountant—to catch him with his guard down. She also feared the pause at the security checkpoint might sap some of her already fragile nerve. When she finally pulled into the gravel parking lot, alongside the rows of colorful yachts, the sun was slanting low behind a thicket of poplars. Greta retrieved the overstuffed binder from the passenger seat, carrying it against her hip with great care, to avoid shedding her evidence. Ingersoll was the sort of man one didn't challenge without tangible, well-substantiated proof. But holding the heavy plastic file at her side, like a battle shield, provided at least a degree of reassurance. She paused at the foot of the slate path that led up to the accountant's club and savored the fresh, invigorating air of the sea. She had lived a landlocked life for many years, far too long. Now this small dose of nature filled her with an inchoate yearning.

The veranda of the boathouse stood nearly empty. In one distant corner of the open deck, a pair of elderly men stared motionless before a chessboard. At the mahogany bar, a heavily-rouged woman in her thirties read a paperback book. Ingersoll waved to Greta from a circular table overlooking the water, where he'd been nursing a cocktail, and he rose from his chair to greet her. The accountant had donned a skipper's cap and a navy blue windbreaker for the occasion. Never before had Greta seen him without a conservative suit and tie, and she was surprised at how robust he appeared. Ingersoll had somehow shed the last vestiges of his lonely yet endearing weariness. Now, he looked genuinely happy. Behind him, cormorants fished noisily off the jetty.

He reached forward to take both of her hands in his. Reluctantly, she set down the plastic binder and the manila envelope on the nearest tabletop.

"I can't believe you're actually here," said Ingersoll. "I know this sounds crazy, Greta, but I was starting to doubt myself. I feared you might have changed your mind."

"I said I'd be here," answered Greta.

If her voice sounded tighter than usual, more matter-of-fact, the accountant didn't seem to notice. He signaled toward a young black waiter in starchy whites, and the man materialized at her side a moment later with a glass of champagne. Ingersoll pressed her to accept it, and she didn't have the fight inside her to refuse. Instead, she drank a toast—"To Betty and George!"—with the con-artist who had swindled her husband. The alcohol singed the back of her throat and burned its way down into her chest.

"Are you ready for our excursion?" asked Ingersoll.

"There's something I want to talk to you about," answered Greta. She steadied herself against the railing of the veranda. "About my taxes. George and my taxes."

"Can't it wait until Monday, Greta?" Ingersoll asked. "I decided not to bring along the returns—to keep this weekend *strictly pleasure*." He leaned toward her, and added, "The only drawback is, technically speaking, we can't write off the trip."

"What I have to say *cannot* wait until Monday," said Greta.

"Oh, then I suppose it can't," agreed the accountant. He suddenly appeared much less certain of himself, and he fiddled with the cuff of his windbreaker. "But there's really nothing to worry about, Greta. I promise you I've gotten you a great deal. Some of the best work I've ever done. Don't you trust me?"

Greta bit into her lip. She could taste the blood—like liquid copper. She looked over Ingersoll's shoulder, at the masts reflecting off the placid water. She examined the black waiter, standing unobtrusively at the far end of the deck. He stared straight forward, not acknowledging her glance. The chess players and the reading woman also paid her no heed. Greta turned once more toward Ingersoll, but kept her eyes focused the far horizon. She consciously averted her gaze from George's treasured binder.

"Would you like my jacket?" Ingersoll offered. "You're shivering."

"George kept photocopies of all our business receipts," she answered.

There. She had said it. She'd set the pebble rolling down the mountainside.

"Photocopies," echoed the accountant. "Did he really?"

Felix Ingersoll smiled down at her nervously. His big dark eyes were tender, desperate, longing—anything but those of a thief. A few more sharp words from her could so easily repay this man for all of his financial antics and could cleave the two of them apart forever. It would serve the bastard right, Greta thought, for what he'd done to her beloved husband. She waited for Ingersoll to say more, but he didn't. His features assumed a guarded pose, his already pale skin turning the color of bone.

"George was very thorough," she continued. "He kept copies of everything."

Greta wanted to say more, to bring down the final boom on whatever there was between herself and the accountant, but something else inside her refused to climb so easily into George's pyre. She swallowed what remained of the champagne, and asked herself what her husband, if he'd been alive to advise her, would have wished her to do. Yet somehow that part of George, the part that could help her make decisions, was no longer accessible. She was on her own now, at least until she decided otherwise. She deposited the empty champagne glass on the whitewashed railing of the veranda.

Ingersoll glanced at the binder; her eyes followed his.

"That's twelve months worth of receipts, right there," said Greta. "I have the rest of them in the trunk of my car—one binder for every year." She weighed each word carefully, sensing that she was steering down a one-way path. All of life was a one-way path, in the end. A constant challenge to choose wisely. Or maybe *choice* had nothing to do with it—maybe each step was inevitable, as certain as death and taxation. "I've been driving around with them all afternoon," she added. "Part of me wishes George hadn't kept copies of everything, you understand. *But he did.*"

"I'm honestly not sure what you mean," replied the accountant. He spoke slowly, as though fearful of choosing the wrong words, but his innocence struck Greta as unconvincing, *so* insincere that he was almost challenging her to embrace it. The two of them stood face to face, eyes locked in mutual scrutiny, each waiting for the other's next move. Ingersoll finally smiled and said, "I do hope nothing is amiss." It was the same tone he'd used, the previous week, inquiring if George were well.

Greta was about to tell him precisely what she meant, exactly what was amiss—to spell out her accusations in harsh, chilling words—when the accountant, without any warning, leaned forward and kissed her on the lips. It was a tender yet powerful gesture, simultaneously gentle and firm. One moment, the man had been standing opposite her, cupping an empty cocktail glass, observing her with anxious eyes, and then, for a brief interlude, the warmth of his mouth pressed against hers. The feeling was one she'd nearly forgotten. Felix Ingersoll drew back quickly, looking sheepish and surprised, but also pleased with himself—like a schoolboy impressed by his own courage. Greta immediately lost track of her charges. Everything that she'd intended to say now felt jumbled, flipped upside down, like a bowl of numbers spun before a lottery drawing. Ingersoll had caught her off guard, once again, this inscrutable man whom she'd trusted, and then did not trust, and now found herself suddenly longing to trust once more. The kiss, so unexpected, also felt so shockingly inevitable. *Of course*, Ingersoll had kissed her. How *couldn't* he have kissed her? Greta reached forward to maintain her balance, and somehow her hand clutched the accountant's sleeve.

"The binders," she said—no longer certain. "We need to talk about the binders."

Ingersoll placed his free hand on top of hers. "Accounting can sometimes be a complex business, full of subtleties and nuances. I do hope you'll give me a chance to explain anything that's troubling you," he said—his voice soothing, as though he was no longer speaking about taxes at all. "You'll do that for me, Greta, won't you?"

"These binders," she said again—and this time the very word *binders* sounded strangely distant to her, like a word in a foreign language that she had once spoken. Why had Ingersoll kissed her like that? What right did he have? She'd intended to say a great deal about the binders, but now all she said was, "I've been driving around with these binders all day, and I'm not sure what to do with them."

She *had* been certain, but every passing moment made her less so. Ingersoll had conned her once more, this time cheating her out of her anger. She wasn't sure how she might recover it—or even whether she wanted to. Instinctively, she placed her free hand on the cover of the bulging plastic binder.

The accountant tightened his grasp on her other hand. "I could dispose of them safely for you," he offered. "If you'd let me."

Greta felt her throat constrict. "It wouldn't be any trouble?"

Ingersoll let out his breath. The remaining tension melted around his eyes and mouth. "I would consider it both a duty and a privilege," he said—his voice as gallant as ever. Then he reached for the binder with both of his hands, sliding it from under hers and slowly elevating the volume over the railing. Greta offered no resistance, watching, waiting. "There you go," he announced, releasing the collection of receipts. "All gone." George's treasure splashed against the water with an eruption of spray and vanished into the depths of the harbor. All that remained, when Greta peered over the balustrade, was a dissipating ripple. As she watched, the breeze gently glazed the water's opaque surface. She looked up only when she felt Ingersoll's hand on her shoulder.

"I *could* take care of the others," he said, "but it will cost you."

She had no opportunity to ask about the price, to absorb fully what Ingersoll had done to her album of tangible evidence. She'd hardly even registered his words before the accountant leaned forward and kissed her again—this time with fresh assurance and vigor. Greta didn't respond, at first, hovering momentarily on the slippery brink of forgiveness. But then she pressed her body firmly into his, accepting all that they would soon share together—the love, the taxes, and life's other, all too certain, inevitabilities.

Rods and Cones

Another family crisis: The rabbit goes blind.

This is not something they've ever thought of losing, the rabbit's vision, not a blow they've braced themselves for, but it happens nonetheless. Suddenly. As though the animal had spied on Lady Godiva through the wire mesh of his hutch. When they return home from work one evening—they've been commuting together, ever since her seizures started—Archimedes is circling the legs of the piano bench. He's anxious, scratching at the carpet and bleating. Every few orbits, he steps nose-first into the trunk of the piano, casting dull reverberations across the living room.

"Are you sure he can't see?" Norm asks. "Both eyes?"

Roberta rocks the bunny in her arms, cradling his head on her bare elbow, running her fingernails gently through his tender beige fur. Poor Archimedes! His tiny heart is dashing; his short plump limbs are quivering with terror. She sways her keychain in front of his nose like a metronome, trying to catch his gaze, but his big slate eyes stare forward into eternal darkness.

"Yes, I'm sure," says Roberta. "What are we going to do?"

"Take him to the vet," says Norm.

That's such a Norm answer. So reasonable that it's unreasonable. Roberta's husband is the senior field engineer at AgroCorp, determined to solve Virginia's problems—and the world's—through hardier sweet corn hybrids.

Norm drapes his windbreaker on the hat tree and removes his tie. A strip of pink flesh separates his hairline from his neckline, evidence of his many hours supervising soil sampling under the bright winter sun. He kisses Roberta on the forehead, between her silver-streaked bangs, and walks into the kitchen. She follows.

"And if the vet can't help?" she says. "*Then* what are we going to do?"

"Then we'll adjust. Blind isn't the end of the world." Norm grins and pours himself a snifter of apple brandy. "Think Stevie Wonder. Ray Charles. Some practice on that piano and we'll have the Ray Charles of rodents."

Roberta nuzzles her cheek against the rabbit's nape. "Are you done?"

"The John Milton of rodents," says Norm. "The Helen Keller of rodents."

"Dammit, Norm. I'm being serious." She releases the rabbit onto the tabletop and watches him scamper for traction along the Formica. "What are we going to *do*?"

"I'm being serious too. Rabbits go blind. What do you want me to say?" He must sense the heat rising behind her eyes, because he adds, "I wouldn't worry too much. I'm sure the vet will figure this out."

.....

The next day is Shrove Tuesday. Roberta knows this, because someone phones the reference desk from a local college bar—at eleven o'clock in the morning!—to ask whether a shrove is an evergreen species or a nickname for pancakes. She's forced to wear her wool coat all morning, since the furnace in the library is still busted. By noon, thinking about the poor blind rabbit trapped in his hutch—they don't dare give him free range of the house anymore, afraid he might topple down the stairs—Roberta grows nauseous. Her eyelids feel swollen from an acute, unshakeable depression. She splashes cold water onto her face, and asks Joyce, the children's librarian, to drive her to the vet.

"Norm is supposed to go with me tomorrow," she explains. "But I don't think I can hold out that long. What if there's a fire and he's stuck in that cage?"

"Don't think twice, honey," says Joyce.

The children's librarian is a big-boned African-American woman about ten years younger than Roberta. She has a son in third grade and a severely autistic daughter. Her second husband—a Filipino chiropractor she met in a support group—has an autistic son and identical twin daughters who play competitive chess. Photos of all five children are Scotch-taped to the dashboard of the librarian's station wagon. "Feel free to push back the seat," says Joyce. "The girls ride in the back and their legs keep growing."

"I'm so sorry about all this," Roberta apologizes. "After we pick up the rabbit, you can just drop me off at the vet. I'll take the bus home."

"Nonsense. Don't you even *think* that again," says Joyce. "You look good, by the way. Are you feeling better these days?"

Roberta knows her colleague is referring to the seizures. The lapses came on without warning, the first attack three years earlier, when they drove Cheyenne up to Vassar. Nothing too serious—just a sparkling of red light followed by a transient absence. Enough to keep her off the streets, but not to kill her. Cause entirely unknown. Dr. Sapir called them pseudoseizures, because they didn't appear on her EEG. He'd recommended a psychiatrist. "I believe you when you say they feel real," he'd said sympathetically. "Somatoform disorders can *feel* as real as genuine physical ailments." He'd given Roberta the name of a leading specialist. But she'd taken the card with the head-shrinker's phone number and slid it into a sewer grate. Hadn't she raised two gifted children and a rabbit while working fulltime? A shrink! Really.

Roberta realizes that Joyce is speaking to her, in need of directions.

"You okay, honey?" asks Joyce. "You're not having an attack, are you?"

Roberta bites into her lip, drawing blood. "No, I'm fine. Just stressed. Say, Joyce, have you ever imagined what it would be like to be blind and a rabbit?"

"Not once," answers Joyce. "I have a hard enough time imagining being me."

.....

The vet's office is located just past the Golden Goose Shopping Center on the Fredericksburg Pike, in a stand-alone building that looks like a big red barn. It shares an L-shaped parking area with a Reformed synagogue and a pediatric dentist. Inside, the atmosphere smells of cat litter and grass pellets and countless varieties of animal fur, all of this blanketed with the sharp stench of antiseptic. Posters pinned to the corkboard walls warn against feline AIDS and heartworm. A chubby boy is waiting in one of the vinyl-coated Barcelona chairs with a ferret in his lap. The ferret looks dead. A plastic carrying case stands open nearby on the linoleum. Otherwise, Roberta and Joyce are the only patrons. When they enter, Dr. Rostow's scarlet macaw, Jezebel, greets them from her elevated cage with a screeching, "Welcome! Peace! Love! Welcome!" Roberta can feel the effect on Archimedes' pulse.

"I know we don't have an appointment," Roberta tells the receptionist. "Do you think Dr. Rostow could please squeeze us in?"

The woman is in her twenties and has piercings through her chin, nose and both eyebrows. Probably other places too. She stands up without acknowledging Roberta, crosses to the far counter, and returns with a clipboard. "Dr. Rostow's not here today," she says. "Her father-in-law had a stroke."

"Oh," says Roberta. "I'm sorry."

"He was young, too—younger than you are." She says this matter-of-fact, with no indication that it might be offensive. "Dr. Pusey is covering for her."

The receptionist says the substitute's name as though Roberta should be grateful. As though Pusey is the Ray Charles of veterinarians.

"And he can squeeze us in?" asks Roberta.

The woman makes a notation on the clipboard. "Take a seat."

"Take a seat," cries the macaw. "Take a load off. Take a breather."

So Roberta sits down. Joyce removes a paperback novel from her purse and reads. The book is titled *Passion Among The Oysters*. Twenty minutes later, Roberta and Archimedes are ushered into the examination room. The boy with the moribund ferret is still waiting in the lobby.

"Blind," says Dr. Pusey. "Goodness. We'll have to do something about that."

The stand-in vet is Dr. Rostow's uncle: a stunningly handsome man in his late fifties, wearing a bowtie and red suspenders. His accent is strong, but not southern. Close, though. Maybe Puritan Yankee: a reassuring voice of the Berkshires or the Maine woods. His features are large and truly grand, like those on the busts of colonial-era statesman. All in all, he exudes an avuncular confidence that announces: "No chaos of the modern world, no malady of rabbits or ferrets, is too much for my time-honored methods." If Roberta were ever going to have an extramarital affair, it would be with a man like Simon Pusey, DVM. But Roberta knows deep down that she will never cheat on Norm.

"They look clear," says Dr. Pusey. He shines the penlight into Archimedes' pupils. "I don't see anything cancerous or ulcerated. How quickly did this happen?"

"It was completely sudden," says Roberta.

Or at least it had *seemed* sudden. But how can she be certain? After all, Archimedes has always been a clever fellow. First prize winner in the "bushy-tailed & floppy-eared" division at the Spotsylvania County Fair—with the royal purple ribbons and the proclamation from the state's agriculture commissioner to prove it. Who was to say he hadn't been concealing his visual decline for months? Or even years. Roberta's mother had been illiterate her entire life—Grandma Bonnie couldn't read a permission slip or a cookie recipe—but she'd kept it from the world until her husband died. Roberta also had a second cousin who'd fled an arson-for-hire prosecution in the 1940s; the family found out only after he suffered a massive aneurysm at sixty-seven and his kids applied for his Medicare. So everyone has secrets. Badges of shame they carry around under heavy clothing. Why should Archimedes be any different?

"I can run some additional tests," says Dr. Pusey. "If you'd like, I can send you for an MRI. But to tell you the truth, Mrs. Koenig, these eyes look fine."

"How can they be fine? He can't see."

"It is a puzzle, isn't it?" says the vet. "This happens, sometimes. After a shock or an injury. If we're lucky, it will clear up on its own."

"But he hasn't had a shock. Honestly, *nothing* has happened. Nothing!"

"Nothing you can see, Mrs. Koenig," says Dr. Pusey. "What's shocking to you might not be shocking to a rabbit. And vice versa."

Roberta is now certain she would have an extramarital affair with Simon Pusey, DVM, if she were the affair-having type. Which she is not. She leaves his office with a referral for an MRI and a pit of anxiety in her abdomen.

.....

That evening, she phones her children to share the bad news. Gabriel is a third-year resident in thoracic surgery at Massachusetts General Hospital. He's the one who bought the rabbit originally—at auction, for three hundred dollars—to impress his high school girlfriend. Roberta still runs into the girl on occasion. Jeanine Farber. She lives with another woman in Fredericksburg, a much older woman, and together they operate a shelter for pregnant teenagers. How strangely life works out sometimes! The girlfriend is long forgotten; the rabbit joins the family. But to Roberta's dismay, Gabriel is only marginally interested in Archimedes. "I'm post-call," he says. "I just fished two explosive bullets out of a toddler's lung. I can't really worry about the rabbit tonight." Cheyenne is even less sympathetic. She's a junior, majoring is field ecology. "Get a grip, Mom," she says. "Millions of children die each year of starvation and cholera. Do you know how many mosquito nets you could buy for that MRI?" And it's true. What her daughter fails to understand is that Roberta doesn't give a damn about the babies vomiting to death in Africa. Not while Archimedes can't see. She has only one rabbit—only one family—and she's entitled to protect it.

Roberta's husband comes down to the kitchen in his boxer shorts. He finds her nursing a cup of hot cocoa. It is after midnight. Crick's *Textbook of Clinical Ophthalmology* and Picardo's *Eye Diseases* lay open on the tabletop. She has also printed out several articles on rabbit vision from the Internet. She likes Dr. Pusey, personally, but she's not going to let Archimedes remain blind on one veterinarian's opinion. "Did you know that rabbits' eyes are mostly rods?" she asks. "Human eyes contain cone-shaped receptors too. That's why we can see color, but they see only black and white."

Norm steps behind her and massages her shoulders.

"That's nice," she says.

"Haven't you had enough medical school for one night?" he asks.

"I'm learning a lot. We should have been checking his tear ducts every week. Tear overflow is often the first sign of underlying pathology."

Norm lets go of her shoulders. "I'll keep that in mind," he says. "I bet I know something about rabbits that's not in any of these book. . . . Do you know how to make a rabbit float?"

"How?" Roberta asks mechanically.

"Pour soda, syrup, and milk into a glass. Add one rabbit."

Roberta says nothing. The sound of scraping rises from Archimedes' hutch, and she rushes toward him. Of course, he's awake. Without eyesight, how can he tell night from day? She strokes his rump, then pours sugar water into a bowl on the mahogany sideboard and lets him lap it up. This reminds her of waking in the wee hours of the morning to nurse Gabriel and Cheyenne. Back when she was too busy to figure out what she wanted in life, but when it didn't matter, because the time in front of her seemed infinite. "We should have planned ahead for this," she says. "We should have had a serious program of ocular hygiene."

"And maybe insurance," says Norm. "You know: Fire, auto, rabbit vision."

"Fuck you," says Roberta.

"Jesus, Roberta. I'm sorry the rabbit can't see. Honestly. But it *is* just a rodent. Not a human being. Don't you think you're taking this a bit too hard?"

She knows that Norm has a point—that rabbits aren't people—but somehow the eyesight of this particular rabbit is essential. And it isn't just the rabbit's eyesight. It's her husband's attitude toward the rabbit's eyesight. *His resignation to the blindness.* The blindness itself is symptomatic. She is married to a man who chuckles off tragedy, be it hers or the rabbit's—who finds pleasure in miniscule accomplishments while life around him falls to hell in a handbasket. Her husband used to breed better sweet corn in order to feed the world; now he just breeds it to produce better sweet corn.

"Let's not argue over this," says Norm. "Be reasonable."

"Rabbits aren't rodents," she answers. "They're lagomorphs."

.....

The MRI is scheduled for the following Friday. That's much too long, as far as Roberta is concerned, to leave the poor rabbit at home alone. She takes off a day from the library, then another. This way, there's no need to lock the animal in his cage. Instead, she follows Archimedes from room to room—guarding against staircases, removing rocking chair runners and electrical cords from his path. Sometimes, if he looks bored, she tries to raise his spirits with a clown-shaped squeak toy or a ball of twine. At lunchtime, she dices him a fine salad of carrots and leeks, seasoned with alfalfa tablets. When he naps, which he does with increasing frequency, she composes a list of all of the blind people she knows. A former co-worker of Norm's, injured in a chemical fire. The retired boxer who mans the counter at the tuxedo-rental shop. Two visually-impaired sisters she went to junior high school with. Amy and Annie Talbot. The older one, the pretty one, did an oral report on Stargardt's disease in eighth grade. The younger one, the ugly one, locked herself in her parents' garage with the exhaust running. Roberta doesn't know many other sightless people. Not personally.

But now she senses how divided they must be from their able-eyed peers. Separated by an invisible barrier that only the blind can see.

On the second afternoon alone with the rabbit, Roberta looks up "Medicine, Alternative & Complementary" in the yellow pages. She scans the ads for any that mention veterinary services. None do. But eventually she finds a listing for one herbalist, in Warrensburg, Maryland, who promises treatment for "all of life's burdens, woes and ailments, including rashes." Certainly, thinks Roberta, this is broad enough to cover deteriorating vision in rabbits. What does she have to lose? But she doesn't dare ask Norm to drive her. Instead, she takes the forty-mile ride in a taxicab. The fare runs nearly one hundred dollars, round-trip, and she realizes this is ridiculous. But is it any more ridiculous than the eyelid surgeries, or golf lessons, or male escorts, on which other women her age squander far more money? She has worked eighteen years at the library. She is entitled to at least one hour-long cab ride.

The drive is a sad one. Past the sub-developments that were so recently tomato fields and turkey farms. When Roberta was a girl, her father, a Brooklyn-born Bavarian Jew who welded for the naval base at Norfolk, took their entire family on a tour of the battlefields from Manassas to Antietam. This was to make his five daughters feel more "*authentische* southern." Forty years later, the sites still harbor the same vintage cannons and grave markers—heralded by matching brown signs on the interstate. But now they are hemmed in by box stores and bowling alleys, drive-thru liquor stores and solid waste disposal sites and overnight parking compounds for school busses. "Southern" and "Brooklyn"—and probably even Bavarian—aren't so distinguishable. The cab driver talks Roberta's ear off with a story about his wife's kidney dialysis and how much her Parkinson's medications cost. Roberta holds Archimedes tight, trying to shelter him from the jolt of the vehicle.

Dr. Zhang's Earthly Remedies occupies a storefront office between a Kosher butcher shop and a taxidermist's. Instinctively, Roberta covers Archimedes' eyes.

It is nearly three o'clock when she checks in at the front desk, but Dr. Zhang is still out to lunch. Roberta waits in the under-furnished and over-lit reception area, surrounded by other patients beyond the salvation of Western science. Most are women her own age. Flabby, depleted creatures with swollen ankles, blotchy skin, and tightly-curled hair in various shades of dye. They crochet, flip through magazines. Keep to themselves. There is no solidarity among the medically forsaken. One of the women has brought along her daughter, or possibly her granddaughter, a teenager with a deformed jaw; the girl amuses herself by performing tricks on a yo-yo. A faint aroma of buttered popcorn hangs in the air—like in a movie theater—though Roberta can't identify the source. The scent leaves her wistful: She hasn't been out to the movies in years. While she waits for Dr. Zhang, she reads *Watership Down*.

The herbalist returns around three-thirty, sporting a long white coat. Roberta has expected Dr. Zhang to be an elderly Chinese man with a wispy gray beard. Half her own height, steeped in the proverbs of the Ming Dynasty. She is stunned to discover that Zhang is female, thirty-something, pushing five foot ten—and decidedly Mediterranean. A fast-talking, olive-skinned beauty with impeccably sculpted eyebrows. "My late husband's name," explains the herbalist. "I'll save you the trouble of wondering."

"Oh," says Roberta. "Of course."

"People are afraid to ask," says Dr. Zhang. "Sometimes they think I'm just the doctor's assistant." The herbalist steers Roberta into an examination room that looks no different from any other doctor's office. It even has a free-standing scale in one corner and a 'basic first-aid' poster taped above the sink. "Let me ask you: Would you have more confidence in a phytotherapist named Zhang or Valadanakis?"

This strikes Roberta as a trick question. Like: 'Have you stopped cheating on your husband yet?' And she's not exactly sure what a phytotherapist is. She smiles—politely, but noncommittal.

"If I had a sense of humor, I'd have 'the former Sofia Valadanakis' printed in parentheses on my business cards," says Dr. Zhang—speaking as rapidly as Roberta can follow. Almost more rapidly. "But George—that's my late husband—was the one with the sense of humor. And he died of an asthma attack. While snorkeling." The herbalist reveals no emotion, as though discussing a news item. "So now you know far too much about me," she says, scanning the forms that Roberta has just filled out. The onion-skin-and-carbon-paper medical history on which she has written "vision trouble" under PRESENT CONCERN. "And now you. So you're having trouble seeing, Mrs. Koenig?"

"It's not me," says Roberta. "It's him."

She extends the rabbit toward the herbalist like a dinner offering. The practitioner steps away from her. "You are kidding me, aren't you?" says Dr. Zhang. "Did my brothers put you up to this?"

"He's blind," continues Roberta. "Both eyes."

"It's a rabbit," says Dr. Zhang. She sneezes several times. "For Christ's sake."

"It's a *blind* rabbit."

The herbalist wipes her eyes and glares down at Roberta. "I don't know if this is supposed to be some sort of practical joke, but I see absolutely no humor in it. None. I run a highly professional establishment here. Some of my patients ride the bus for hours to see me." She exhales decisively. "Now if you'll excuse me."

Dr. Zhang drops Roberta's folder into a wire basket suspended from the wall and calls through the intercom for her next patient. Then she sneezes again.

"Please, doctor," says Roberta. She has learned long ago that addressing all health professionals as 'doctor'—even dental hygienists—makes them feel important and thus generous. "I'm not here on a prank. I've got a blind rabbit beyond the help of Western veterinary care and I don't know where to turn. Don't you have anything that might work in rabbits?"

The herbalist's expression softens. She examines Roberta's face in silence, as though trying to gauge her sincerity. "Look, Mrs. Koenig. Roberta. I wish I could help you," she finally says. "But my remedies have been tested in human beings for thousands of years. To administer them to house pets—without any history, without any tradition of success—would be irresponsible. I'd be taking advantage of you. Honestly, it would be quackery." The herbalist reaches forward and caresses Archimedes. "I'm sorry. I wish I could help."

"That's alright," says Roberta. "It's not your fault."

She hugs the rabbit to her chest and drags herself toward the door.

"Wait, Roberta," says the herbalist.

"Yes?"

"Would you like something *for you*? To reduce your anxiety," asks Dr. Zhang. "Maybe some valerian extract with passion flower. Or a bundle of kava kava root. Just to tide you over..."

"Thanks," says Roberta. "But no thanks."

She sobs on the long return trip across the snow-patched exurbs, wiping her tears on Archimedes' fur. It has started to rain—an icy drizzle—and the driving turns slow and treacherous. The wipers of the cab produce an unnerving two-pronged snap with every passage across the windshield. Roberta hopes to reach home before Norm returns from work. Desperately. Because she doesn't want him to know about the herbalist. Because she feels guilty, as though she has been trysting.

When the cab drops her off, she finds the house dark and empty. Like a mausoleum. She sits in the kitchen without turning on the lights. She is angry that it is nearly six o'clock and her husband has left her alone with the suffering rabbit.

.....

Norm returns home *much* later than usual.

Roberta is struck by how profoundly tired he appears. And it's not the sort of short-term fatigue that can be cured by a nap, but a deeper and abiding exhaustion. As though he has been excavating his own grave in secret. She feels a rush of tenderness toward him: He may be a potbellied plodder, but he's *her* potbellied plodder.

"Where were you?" she asks.

Her husband pours himself a double brandy. "I went for a drive. Nowhere in particular." He downs his drink quickly and rinses the glass. "Where were *you*?"

"What do you mean?"

"I tried you here. I tried you at the library," says Norm. "I was actually worried."

Why *actually*? Isn't it normal for husbands to be concerned about their wives?

"I must not have heard the phone," says Roberta.

Norm nods. "Okay, I trust you," he says. "You're entitled to some privacy. But I'm not stupid, Roberta. You *always* hear the phone."

He apparently wishes to have a small fight, not an existential one. His faith in her is exasperating.

She considers answering: Oh, and I'm having a torrid affair with our substitute veterinarian. But even lying about an affair is beyond her.

.....

Roberta brings the rabbit with her to work the following Monday. She sets his travel cage on the window bench opposite the atlases, letting his skin soak up the warm morning light. This violates longstanding library policy: All animals other than guide dogs are strictly forbidden. But what are they going to do? Fire her? After eighteen years of immaculate service? Obviously not. When the newly-hired chief librarian, Edith Garly, asks about Archimedes, all Roberta says is that he was struck blind and can't be left home alone. "I suppose not," agrees Roberta's supervisor. "I hope he feels better." When Edith crosses through the reference room again around noon, she offers Archimedes the sliced cucumber from her sandwich.

The new boiler is fully functional now—finally—and the library is bustling. A retired priest enlists Roberta in a genealogy project. For his sister's birthday. Then a high school student asks her for help with the microfiche readers. She is so busy, she nearly forgets what's wrong.

At the end of children's reading hour, Joyce sends her five year olds and their chaperones to visit the new bunny. Roberta insists the kids stay perfectly quiet, but allows them to pet Archimedes' pelt one at a time. "Rabbits have very strong eyesight," whispers a mother with a double chin. "That's why they never wear glasses." Another woman, a Jamaican nanny supervising a blonde child, urges that angelic little girl to make a wish. "Make yourself a *wise* wish, girl," she says. "Life only be giving you so many wishes." After that, all of the other boys and girls demand wishes too. Several of them shout their requests out loud: *I wished for a turtle! I want a submarine!* At the suggestion of the mother with the double chin, the kids then line up outside the handicapped bathroom and wash their hands.

"He sure is one popular bunny," says Joyce.

"Yeah, I guess," says Roberta. But the children's visit has depressed her. Somehow, their enthusiasm makes the adult world's indifference all the more striking. She remembers taking Gabriel and her own late mother, Grandma Bonnie, to see the lambs at the petting zoo in Richmond—while Norm was in graduate school, before Cheyenne was born—and how *that* life has turned into *this* life is inexplicable to her. As mysterious as the rabbit's ailment. "He's thirteen years old and blind," she says. "I'm afraid that his eyes might only be the tip of the iceberg. That he might die."

"I'll pray for him," says Joyce.

"I appreciate that," says Roberta. "Say, Joyce, I hate to do this—but can I hit you up later for another lift?"

"Sure thing. If you don't mind stopping at the chess academy to pick up the girls."

"I want to take the rabbit someplace," Roberta explains, "and I don't want Norm to know."

Joyce puts her arm on Roberta's shoulder. "I'll pray for you, too."

.....

Three hours later, Joyce drops Roberta in front of the veterinarian's office. There are still half a dozen cars in the parking lot—including a Mercedes stationed in the space reserved for the pediatric dentist. Dr. Rostow's spot remains empty. Roberta waves to her departing colleague and then crosses the lot, carrying the rabbit's case in one hand like a valise. She catches her reflection in the mirrored paneling that encircles the foundation of the dentist's office. With her kerchief and rabbit case, she looks like Hollywood's take on that innocent country girl arriving in the big city for the first time. Only older. Much, much older. Fit to star in the AARP's version of *Wonderful Town*. She was once good-looking. Now she is good-looking *for her age*. But at least that is something. Many women aren't good-looking for *any* age. She undoes her kerchief and lets her bangs hang loose. Then she strides quickly into the synagogue.

There is a security officer at the entrance: a small-framed black man in his seventies, more fit to guard an obscure room in an art museum than to ward off Islamic terrorists. He smiles at Roberta, but doesn't ask where she is going. She hasn't been inside a synagogue for many years. Maybe not since her youngest sister's wedding. But she possesses her father's dark features and a matronly suburban look that would open temple doors across the continent.

Roberta follows the blue-and-white carpeting past the racks of folding chairs, the toddler finger-paintings suspended on clothespins, the adjacent American and Israeli flags. Someone is testing the public address system. "Are we on? Are we on? Testing, three-two-one." Then something in Spanish. She wanders down the stairs, searching for the rabbi's office. Instead, she finds herself in the gymnasium. It's not a regulation-size basketball court, but there is a digital scoreboard and a row of tiered wooden bleachers. Incandescent light—far too weak—reflects off chalk-yellow walls. At the far end of the court, an agonizingly lean young man is shooting free-throws. Apparently alone. He is wearing Bermuda shorts and a yarmulke. The gym smells of perspiration and floor wax. In the confined space, the echo of the basketball rings thunderously.

"I'm looking for the rabbi," says Roberta.

The young man braces the loose ball under his foot and wipes his forehead with a face towel. Sweat forms black stains in the armpits of his gray T-shirt. "I'm Rabbi Tate," he says.

"Oh, Jesus," says Roberta. The man must be half her age—or close to it. And then it strikes her: He's probably the same age as her son. Her son who is fishing explosive bullets out of toddlers.

"Would you like to sit down?" asks Rabbi Tate.

Roberta follows him to the first row of bleachers. "Thank you," she says.

"Wow. It's a rabbit," says the rabbi. "May I?"

She nods. The rabbi opens the cage and scratches Archimedes' scruff. "'The rabbits are a feeble folk, but they build strong houses in the rocks,'" he declaims. "Our King Solomon wrote that nearly three thousand years ago. Pretty amazing, huh?"

"I'm not religious," answers Roberta. Then—apropos of nothing: "I'm Roberta Koenig." She pats the rabbit between the ears. "This is Archimedes."

"Good to meet you, Mrs. Koenig, Archimedes," says Rabbi Tate. "Now what can I do for you?"

"You're going to laugh at me, rabbi. But my bunny-rabbit has gone blind. Our family's bunny-rabbit. And I'm looking for—I don't know—spiritual guidance." Roberta lowers her voice. "I know this sounds crazy—but do you think prayer could bring back his eyesight?"

Rabbi Tate frowns intensely. "Is it a Jewish rabbit?"

"Goodness, I don't know. Is that important—?"

"It was a joke, Mrs. Koenig," says Rabbi Tate. "I couldn't resist. Forgive me. There's a similar joke about a St. Bernard wanting a bar mitzvah."

"I'm sorry. I'm not feeling up to jokes."

"It *is* an interesting theological question you raise, though. About the extent of our obligation to bring up house pets in our faith." At first, Roberta suspects the rabbi is still joking with her, but soon she realizes he is quite serious. "Take the issue of *kashrut*, for example. Dietary laws. During the year, according to the Talmud, it is permissible to feed one's pets any food one wishes. Kosher or non-Kosher doesn't matter. If Fido enjoys a shrimp cocktail and a ham-and-cheese sandwich at the end of a long walk, all the power to him." Rabbi Tate fingers Archimedes' ears while he speaks. "But on the Passover, it is expected that one serve one's pets only those foods that are kosher *le Pesach*."

"I see," says Roberta. "What about my rabbit?"

"Prayer certainly can't hurt," the rabbi answers. "As long as you don't expect too much. The Almighty might have a reason for closing your bunny's eyes."

"You mean God *wants* him blind? Like a punishment? I don't believe it."

"Or a reward," says Rabbi Tate. "Let me try an analogy. Often being bumped off an airliner is an inconvenience, but on rare occasions it is a blessing."

"So I *shouldn't* pray?" asks Roberta.

"Quite the opposite, I think," says the rabbi. "*I'd* certainly pray for Archimedes here. May he live to be one hundred twenty with the eyesight of a falcon.... And hopefully God *will* answer your prayers. But if he doesn't, don't despair. Accept that the Almighty may have a good reason for not answering them."

"That makes sense, I think," says Roberta. Though she is not so sure that it does. What is clear to her is that whatever wisdom she is searching for, it is not to be gleaned from this clergyman half her age. In a way, Rabbi Tate reminds her of Norm. Or of the youthful, idealistic Norm she once married. Her fiancé was also continually cracking jokes about St. Bernards wanting bar mitzvahs—and Lord knows what. And it isn't that his jokes are any less funny now, she knows. It's just that losing her parents, and then her children, and then her rabbit's vision, has drained all the humor out of her.

The young rabbi stands up. "I do hope that I've been helpful to you," he says, shaking her hand. "Please come back again. Anytime."

He takes the basketball and shoots from three-point range. His shot misses the backboard by nearly twenty yards.

.....

They go together on Friday for the brain scan. Magnetic imaging for house pets is not a routine matter, so they must drive all the way to Washington. To District Animal Services—a specialized facility located on Connecticut Avenue, between the National Zoo and the Braille Museum. Norm is vocally unhappy about taking off a full day from work. He hasn't skipped more than a morning since his father died. But Roberta has been adamant that a hundred-dollar cab fare would be ludicrous.

She rides in the back seat with the rabbit. When Archimedes dozes off, she takes a small notebook out of her purse.

Norm glances at her through the rearview mirror. "What are you doing?" he asks.

"Do you really want me to tell you?" she says. "I'm making a list of all the dead people I know."

She is actually doing it, too. Starting with her grandparents and working her way forward in rough chronological order. Her elementary school teachers, her Girl Scout troupe leaders, blind Annie Talbot. Then her college suitemates—both of them. Her children's piano tutor. Her first mentor at the library. It is a far longer list than the list of blind people. A history of her own existence, told through obituaries. Roberta feels as though she could spend the entire rest of her life listing these names and never be finished.

"Please don't be that way," says Norm.

She adds the name of her ex-hair stylist to the death list. "What way?"

Norm tries to meet her eyes in the mirror, but she looks away. "Are you sure you wouldn't rather talk about rods and cones, or something?" he asks.

This may be the last thing on earth she wants to talk about. Now.

"Good God," she snaps. "You can't just start talking about rods and cones one day when you don't know the first thing about them. When you haven't paid any attention to them for your entire goddam life. How would you feel if I said: 'Let's talk about sweet corn'?"

"Well, okay then," says Norm. "I won't mention it again."

"You know nothing about rods and cones," she shouts. "*You* could have rods instead of cones, Norm, and you'd never even know it."

"Maybe," agrees Norm. "You're probably right."

.....

The animal hospital is a steel-and-cinderblock structure shaped like an upside down ice cream cone. An architectural landmark of the 1970s. Radiology & Imaging is located on the 14th Floor. Opposite nephrology. The two specialties share a common waiting area, so the table brochures include tips on canine kidney transplantation and post-dialysis instructions for domestic cats. The patients of various species, Roberta suddenly realizes, are segregated by appointment times. Everyone in the waiting area that morning—and it is a teeming office, like something out of a North African marketplace—carries an ailing rabbit just like hers.

They are assigned a number by a male technician sporting aquamarine scrubs. 1313. It is difficult to believe that one thousand three hundred and twelve house pets have been imaged ahead of them. "We're running behind," the technician explains in a high-pitched, singsong voice. "But I promise we'll get to you. I don't go home until you do."

So they wait. All through the morning, all through the afternoon. Roberta is used to this. She has been in and out of waiting rooms for two weeks already. And it often feels as though she has been waiting her entire life. For plumbers, for carpools. Maybe she has acquired an immunity. When she finishes *Watership Down*, she turns back to page three and starts the novel over again. Without thinking twice. But Norm grows antsy, irritable. He is *not* used to waiting. He cracks several jokes—far too loud—about how long it will take for the stew to boil. The other rabbit owners give him dirty looks and shield their pets.

"Thirteen thirteen," croons the technician. "Two un-luckies make a lucky."

"*Two un-luckies make a lucky*," mocks Norm under his breath.

"Sorry for the delay," says the tech. "We only have one machine."

What follows is the most thorough veterinary check-up that Roberta has ever witnessed. Two specialists examine Archimedes from the points of his floppy ears down to the bristles of his bushy tail. Then they shake hands with her and Norm, and hand the three of them off to another technician. The second technician is also male, wearing aquamarine scrubs, but this one sports bunny slippers.

The MRI itself is anticlimactic. One nurse injects a sedative above Archimedes' hind leg and another straps him onto a concave gurney.

"This part is easy," says the technician. "Just like making toast."

Then he slides the incapacitated animal into a device that does indeed resemble a futuristic toaster oven.

A long beep. Two short beeps. Another long beep. That's it.

Out comes rabbit and gurney and all.

"Like toast, see," says the technician. "Results in two weeks."

Roberta imagines this is some sort of magic trick. That their technician will have pulled a fully-sighted rabbit out of the toaster. But that doesn't happen, of course. When Archimedes wakes up from his sedation, he is still blind.

.....

The rabbit sleeps fitfully on the ride home, through outbound rush-hour traffic. Archimedes has had a long, exhausting day. His brow feels feverish. Roberta worries that he may be clinically depressed. She is also concerned that it is unsafe to ride with the animal loose on her lap. That an accident will catapult him through the windshield. But what alternative is there? She has searched the Internet for rabbit car seats, but once again the technology lags behind the need. She wants to ask Norm to drive carefully, but she knows this will spawn an argument. And she is far too worn down for any more fighting. It is as though something deep inside her—something tiny yet essential, like the heart of a rabbit—has turned to marble.

They hardly speak on the drive home. When they pull into the driveway, twilight has already descended over the bare hedges. A damp chill clings to the air. It is mid-March, but it is hard to imagine that spring lurks just around the corner. Roberta carries the sleeping rabbit into the house, as she once did with Gabriel and Cheyenne after long car trips. Her husband follows with the carrying case. He tries to turn on the chandelier in the foyer, but the bulbs have burnt out. All three of them. Undaunted, he flips on the table lamp in the living room. Meanwhile, Roberta gathers the pillows of the sofa together into a small mound, creating a soft, snug nest for Archimedes.

Norm walks into the kitchen and returns with a glass and the brandy bottle. He fills the snifter nearly halfway.

"What a day," he says—as though nothing is out of the ordinary. "If we're lucky, the MRI will show something and we'll know what to do next."

"It won't show anything," says Roberta.

Her husband sips his brandy. "You don't know that," he says.

"I know that."

"Okay, you know that," says Norm. "I won't argue with you. But I think we should have a serious talk, Roberta." Her husband pauses, either searching for words or for courage. "Before this lagomorph damages our marriage."

"*Before* it damages our marriage?! Oh Norman, it's not just the rabbit—" she says. But then she doesn't say anything else. Not a word. The red sparkling lights flash before her eyes, and the room peels away. This time she hears bells, buzzers, whistles. She pictures herself adding her own name to the list of dead people she knows. Roberta Lynn Koenig. And then she sees her husband reading the list, arriving at her name, and weeping. She senses the passage of time: minutes, a quarter of an hour. When she comes to, Norm is holding her clammy hand. Pressing his lips into the base of her palms. And he does have tears in his eyes. "Please, Roberta, darling. Wake up," he begs.

She looks up at him and smiles groggily. "I'm awake," she says. "I think."

Then she looks across the sofa. And there is the rabbit. Looking toward her. Looking *at* her. She lifts her arm—and his big slate eyes follow.

"He can see," she shouts. "Oh, Norm. He can see! *He can see!*"

"I'll be damned," says Norm. "I think you're right."

And they sit there, holding hands like a solid and inescapably married couple, the rabbit staring back at them both in utter bewilderment.

The Extinction of Fairytales

Edie Crossgrove liked to say that she'd inherited Sammy from the previous owners of the house. That had been in the summer of (*Good heavens! How time evaporated!*) 1967, the summer the race war threatened to tear the very mortar out of the democratic brickwork. Edie had been on a stepladder in the breakfast nook—laying shelving paper in her new cupboards, mulling over a fresh theory regarding Old Mother Hubbard—when a lanky young black man appeared on the kitchen steps and rapped his knuckles on the storm door. He leaned forward at the shoulders in a permanent hunch, the sort of deformity a laborer might develop from years stooped over a vacuum cleaner, or a leaf blower, but that also might come from serving well-off white people. When he finished knocking, he removed his tweed cap and held it to his chest with both hands. Edie could not imagine what business this man had at her back door, but he seemed quite the opposite of the lanky young black men burning up Detroit and Newark, so she put on her slippers and steered her course between cartons of newspaper-shrouded glassware. Her baby-girl Rhodesian ridgeback, Hans Christian Andersen, lumbered after her. It was a torrid afternoon, matted with pollen and the scent of tea roses.

"Yes?" asked Edie, propping the storm door open several inches.

"I'm here to mow the lawn," said the young man.

"Oh, I see," echoed Edie. "You're here to mow the lawn." She'd been in the house only ten days, and it hadn't crossed her mind that grass needed to be cut regularly, that it didn't simply stop growing when it reached the appropriate height—like puppies or children. "Very well," she said. "Mow the lawn."

The young man remained on the porch. He shuffled his feet nervously, his eyes downcast. The sun reflected off an unpleasant scar that ran from his Adam's apple to the base of his left ear. He reminded Edie of a shy bellhop waiting for a tip—and that's when she realized he wanted to agree upon the price. Of course. But what did one pay a grown adult to tend one's lawn? Edie didn't wish to appear cheap, but she'd just purchased a twenty thousand dollar suburban home on a freelance folklorist's income. She had far more uncut grass than she had money to spare.

"I'll pay you twelve dollars," said Edie. "In advance."

Some of the tension melted from the man's shoulders. "Mrs. Tidings, ma'am, she paid me eight."

"Well, I'm not Mrs. Tidings," said Edie. "I'll pay you twelve."

"Thank you, ma'am," he said.

"Let me just find my purse . . ."

"That's all right, ma'am," he said. "Sammy trusts you. Nobody's never run off on me with a lawn." Sammy grinned. "Lawns don't travel none too well."

Edie smiled back—to be polite, to seal the bargain. And that was that.

Every other Tuesday, for thirty-seven years, Sammy's van pulled up at the curbside, loaded with mowers and blowers and clippers. He'd gone through a series of used vehicles over the decades—first a taupe DeSoto with corroded bumpers, then a cortege of Dodges and Plymouths—but he never once skipped work on account of car trouble. (Although for a stretch he did squeeze his hand-mower sideways into a station wagon that he'd borrowed from his sister's husband.) In the autumn, he cleared the leaves and helped Edie plant bulbs. In the winter, he shoveled snow. On those winter mornings when there was no snow, Edie wasn't sure exactly what he did—but she paid him anyway, much like keeping a lawyer on retainer.

As the years passed, Sammy's stoop grew increasingly pronounced. When Edie glanced out the kitchen window, her employee was often slumped so far over the riding mower that only the vehicle's turns reassured her that he was still alive. What remained of his hair, a frail monk's ring, faded to a ghostly white. While he didn't smoke—or at least Edie had never seen him smoking—Sammy developed a deep, brassy cough that filled many a checkered handkerchief with phlegm. Yet he never phoned in sick. Not once. Nor did he excuse himself for deaths or illnesses in his family. As far as Edie knew, he'd never even taken a vacation, a suspicion at least partly confirmed after the terrorist attacks of 9-11, when Sammy admitted that he hadn't ever flown in an airplane. (He called it an "aero-plane.") But at twelve dollars per lawn—his rates never changed over a third of a century—who could possibly afford a vacation?

So Sammy grew older. And Edie grew older. Her ankles swelled; her joints throbbed. One night a clot of blood broke free from her heart-wall and plugged up the left side of her brain. Meanwhile, the row of black birches that Sammy had planted for her alongside the property line developed into saplings, then full-fledged trees, until one crashed onto Edie's VW during a gale, and the rest acquired fungal cankers and had to be destroyed. The aging gardener (*Who knew if Sammy were fifty-five or seventy!*)—arrived each week in the same bib overalls, his massive hands sporting the same padded jersey gloves, his broad face smiling eternally like an early Christian martyr in pain.

And then, one day, he didn't show up.

.....

At first, Edie hardly noticed. She'd been so worn down after the stroke, so frustrated trying to write with her left hand, that it wasn't until Wednesday afternoon that she realized Tuesday had come and gone without Sammy. But even then, she didn't think much of it. Emergencies came up, after all. Tires blew out. Teeth chipped. Past sixty, if it wasn't something it was something else. Besides, there was no denying that a single absence in thirty-seven years was a mighty fine track record—the sort of accomplishment you might phone in to one of those morning radio programs—so she wasn't complaining. But when a second week went by without any sign of Sammy, Edie began to grow concerned. It dawned on her that he might be ill or incapacitated—or (*God forbid!*) something worse. She hoisted herself onto her newly-installed staircase lift, thinking she would telephone him from the extension in the kitchen. It wasn't until she opened her address book that she grasped that she had no contact information for Sammy. No address, no phone number, nothing. They'd always conducted their business face-to-face—the old-fashioned way. As ridiculous as it seemed, Edie suddenly discovered that she didn't even know Sammy's last name.

She dialed the operator. "Operator? Yes, the surname is Tidings. Julius Tidings.... Or possibly Jerome." But Dr. Tidings had been pushing seventy when she'd bought the house from him—that would make him... one hundred seven years old. "Scratch that. Would you please try a Maggie Tidings, maybe Margaret... I honestly don't know. Can't you check the whole metro area?" Mrs. Tidings had been considerably younger, a fragile woman who wore her auburn hair up in a pompadour. If anybody would know about Sammy, she would. "Oh, you don't," said Edie. "I see. No, that's all." She hung up the phone, on the verge of panic. What sort of woman had she been all these years that she didn't know the last name of her own gardener? Had she really been so—oblivious?

When Edie had purchased the house in East Salem, with the bulk of her father's insurance money, her friends had scoffed. Back then, single women didn't buy three-bedroom suburban homes on their own. But after her parents' accident—they'd won a ski vacation in a sweepstakes and been crushed by an avalanche—she wanted to grow up quickly. Already, at Vassar, she'd found her life's calling. Nursery rhymes. Fairy tales. Why not have a solid home-base from which to conduct her research undisturbed? So what if the neighbors thought her peculiar. (*And hadn't they thought her peculiar! Surgeons and orthodontists who reminded her of Charles Bovary.*) It was only now, crippled, isolated, that she second-guessed herself. Why hadn't she ever offered Sammy a raise? Why hadn't she taken an interest in his life? She couldn't let him disappear like her parents had—leaving all of those unanswered and unanswerable questions. Yet the more she thought about it, the more she understood that she knew virtually nothing about him. She didn't know where he lived. Or if he were married. All she knew was that he had a sister whose husband had once owned a weather-beaten station wagon.

During those early days of Sammy's absence, Edie sat at the bay windows in the living room and watched the street for his van. Each approaching vehicle raised and then dashed her expectations, as though her mood were harnessed to a passing siren. She knew the situation called for action—drastic action—but what? Phone the police and tell them that her gardener had disappeared? They'd indulge her just long enough to stash their report in a cylindrical filing cabinet. She considered putting up flyers, wheeling herself door-to-door in the hope that Sammy had mowed other lawns in the area. Another possibility was placing an advertisement in the local paper. Yet each of these options struck her as somehow unacceptable—humiliating, quite frankly—and while she desperately wanted Sammy back, she wasn't about to beg publicly for his return. Besides, what if he'd once committed a petty crime, like stealing a pork-chop, and had been on the lam all these years? Her advertisement might bring the law down on him. No, far better to wait. She would work on her manuscript and he would return.

Edie was up to revising her chapter on "Lucy Locket":

> *Lucy Locket lost her pocket,*
> *Kitty Fisher found it;*
> *There was not a penny in it,*
> *Only ribbon round it.*

When Edie was a girl, every school kid had known that verse—although probably not that Lucy Locket was a gold-digging English barmaid who'd passed her lovers onto actress-prostitute Kitty. Now, both rhyme and reason had been long forgotten. Or nearly forgotten, relegated to the memories of a few old souls like Edie. That's what her book was all about—preserving these fading fables and rounds and limericks. A challenging enough project under the best of circumstances, not rendered any easier by the grief of Sammy's disappearance. It became nearly impossible when that noxious woman next door—the same meddlesome creature who was always on her case about hiring a homecare attendant—began pestering Edie about the lawn.

.....

"—And I use the term lawn generously," said Liz. "What you have now might properly be called a meadow. My husband says it's a fire hazard—and he was trained as an engineer, so if anyone should know, he should."

Liz served as the language arts coordinator at a local elementary school—in theory a lover of words—but the similarities between her and Edie stopped there. The program she administered taught American kids traditional African songs and Aborigine bedtime stories. To Liz Blatch, this multiculturalism embodied progress. To Edie, it was linguistic pollution by a saccharine name. Not that there was anything wrong with African music or Aborigine bedtime stories—indeed, they ought to be preserved and treasured—but not scattered haphazardly like some sort of cultural seasoning. Liz's work was the folkloric equivalent of spreading an invasive species, or of interbreeding purebred dogs. But what could you expect from a woman who wore maroon toe-polish and a medical alert bracelet shaped like a valentine?

"There's no need to exaggerate," said Edie. "It's only been a month or so."

"It's been at least six weeks," retorted Liz. "I don't mean to give you a hard time, Miss Crossgrove, but you could graze sheep out there. A child could trip and die in that grass, and nobody would notice."

Edie pulled her blanket over her knees. It was nearly ninety degrees outside, but ever since the stroke, she'd suffered perpetual chills. "I thought you didn't have any children," said Edie.

"That's not the point."

"By the time you have children," said Edie, "I'll have the lawn mowed."

They were in the parlor, a dimly-lit catacomb of curios and knickknacks gathered on Edie's fairytale-hunting expeditions. Liz rose from the sofa and reseated herself on the sagging loveseat beside Edie's wheelchair. She reached forward, as though to touch her hostess's arm, but drew back. "I don't want to sound presumptuous," said Liz—in a tone she might use to warn a third grader who lacked permission to visit the restroom—"but don't you think it might be better if there were someone to look after you?"

"Are you volunteering?" snapped Edie.

This caught the young educator off-guard. "Well, I could certainly help *find* someone . . . I mean . . ."

"I'm doing quite alright on my own, thank you," said Edie. "My only problem is that Sammy—the man who mows my lawn—has gone missing."

That perked Liz up. "That's all. Why didn't you say so? I'm sure if I spoke to our Julio, he'd be able to squeeze you in—and he's not too pricey at all—"

"I'm waiting for Sammy to come back."

Liz toyed with her wedding ring. "How long do you expect that will be?"

Edie shrugged. "As long as it takes."

"Now, really, Mrs. Crossgrove—"

"You heard me, dear. *I'm waiting for Sammy to come back.*"

Edie considered trying to explain the matter further—but there was no way to teach the whole of life to a woman half her age. Anything she said would somehow make her relationship with Sammy sound illicit.

"What's Julio like?" Edie asked.

"What's he *like*?" repeated Liz. "I don't know. I think he's Peruvian. . . . And very reliable. . . . Are you sure you don't want me to send him over tomorrow?"

"Oh, absolutely not," answered Edie—her tongue loosened by age and stroke. "I just wanted to check if you were sleeping with him."

. . . . .

Sammy had only been inside Edie's house once. She'd come back early from swimming at the municipal pool—it must have been that first summer after she moved in—and he'd just finished trimming the weeds that were continually poking up between the flagstones on the patio. Maybe because he knew she wasn't home, Sammy had taken off his t-shirt and tied it around his neck like a bandanna. His chest hairs were coarse and irregular. Edie wore only her bathing suit, a two-piece she'd purchased in college on a whim. While they stood together, appraising Sammy's handiwork, the sky went overcast. A hard breeze raised the gooseflesh on Edie's arms. Then rain started falling in enormous beads, splattering on the deck like bird eggs dropped from a height.

"My heavens," exclaimed Edie. "We're in for a show."

The clouds pulsed with light and—after a short interval—rolled with thunder. Hans Christian Anderson yelped and cowered in the privet.

"Two miles away," said Sammy.

"What's that?"

"Don't you know about thunder-counting, Miss Crossgrove? You take the number of seconds between the lightning and thunderclap, and you cut that number in half, and half-again—and then you know how far away the storm is sitting."

"I didn't know that," said Edie. "You'd better come inside before you get soaked."

She darted up the kitchen stairs. Sammy held back. He stood just beyond the porch eaves, getting whipped by wind and water.

"Come on," called Edie.

Sammy looked up at the sky and wiped a sheet of water off his brow. "I suppose that would be okay."

Inside, Edie handed him a bath towel and poured him out a cup of tea. She slipped into her bathrobe. "You might as well hunker down until it blows over," she said. "No use catching pneumonia."

Sammy waited awkwardly beside the table. The tea cup stood untouched, sending off a brew of vapor.

"You all right?" she asked.

"Sure thing, Miss Crossgrove. I just—well—some folks wouldn't want me in their house like this."

Did he mean shirtless? Or did he mean as a black man?

"Oh," said Edie. "Wouldn't they?"

The words sounded wrong as soon as she said them. Either naïve or flirtatious, somehow the opposite of reassuring. Luckily, Sammy caught sight of the books on the table and diverted the conversation.

"Baby books," he said.

He tentatively leafed through the topmost volume.

"Not mine," objected Edie. "Or, rather, they're mine—but not in that way. It's what I do for a living."

Sammy looked up curiously. "You're a writer, Miss Crossgrove?"

"Oh, no. I study children's stories—fairy tales, nursery rhymes. They're going extinct, I'm afraid. Each generation knows fewer and fewer... I'm tracking their disappearance."

Sammy nodded. She sensed he had absolutely no idea what she was talking about—that she might just as well have said that she earned her keep by weighing angels.

"Do you know any nursery rhymes?" she asked.

"Miss Crossgrove?"

"Like *Peter Peter Pumpkin Eater*," she suggested, "or *Ride a cock horse to Banbury Cross?*"

He returned the book to the stack. "I'm sure I don't remember."

"How about fairy tales?" persisted Edie.

Sammy shrugged. "I'm too old for fairy tales." Their eyes met and then he looked away quickly. "I think I'm through for the morning, Miss Crossgrove..."

"Oh, certainly," agreed Edie—rummaging through her "business cabinet" for the envelope with his twelve dollars.

She had the good sense not to invite him inside again.

.....

But now she wished she had. Her inability to connect with Sammy—to transcend race, class, whatever—now struck her as one of her greatest failures. What made it worse was that in the field, on a fairytale hunting mission to Micronesia or Kamchatka or Appalachia, she'd have culled his childhood memories out of him over the course of hours, pressed him politely but firmly until she wore down his defenses. Yet in her own home, at her own kitchen table, she'd accomplished nothing. After thirty-seven years, she hadn't learned enough about Sammy to fill an index card. Or maybe she's learned a great deal about Sammy, everything she needed to know, but none of it was the sort of tangible knowledge you could catalogue like a nursery rhyme or make use of in a missing-persons search.

.....

It wasn't quite true that Sammy had never been inside the house again. He'd been in the vestibule briefly, on that morning fifteen years later, when Edie had come down the stairs to find Hans Christian Anderson curled up dead beside the umbrella stand. She'd opened the front door and waited in the entryway, her entire body quivering. It wasn't just the loss of the dog that unsettled her—as horrid as that was—but somehow also the reminder that the ridgeback was all she had. No husband. No children. (*By choice, of course—*

Who wanted to spend a lifetime changing diapers and washing laundry and shaking out rectal thermometers?—But still!) All Edie had now was a puppy who was now seventeen years old and lifeless. She leaned into the open closet, hiding herself among the heavy old coats as she'd done as a girl. The scent of her Mama was still trapped in the faux-fur linings. "I want her back," she screamed into the fabric. She wasn't sure whether she was thinking of her mother or her dog. Edie was still screaming when Sammy stepped into the foyer.

"Miss Crossgrove?" he asked tentatively.

He removed his cap and stashed it in his pocket.

"Oh, Sammy," she said. "Do you know how Chicken Little feels when the sky starts falling? I feel like that now . . ."

Sammy turned on the hall lights and spotted the cadaver.

"It's gonna be alright, Miss Crossgrove," he said. "Sammy's gonna take care of everything." He scooped the dog up in his arms and carried her limp body across the threshold with all the tenderness of a bridegroom. Edie followed him, almost robotically. "Do you have anything to wrap her up in?" asked Sammy.

Edie didn't answer. She realized she was still wearing her nightgown. It didn't come halfway down her thighs, but Sammy wasn't looking.

"I know what we'll do," he said. "I've got just the thing."

He carried the lifeless form to the curbside and deposited it gently on the grass. Then he slid open the side-door of his van and started removing books from a wooden crate. "Bibles. For my church," he explained. "But if they're good enough for the Good Book, I suppose they're good enough for Miss Andersen." (*Only Sammy could call an old, dead dog by her last name!*)

"Thank you," said Edie—her voice barely audible.

"No need to cry," soothed Sammy while he set the body into the makeshift coffin. "Miss Andersen's done her duty. She's earned her rest." He replaced the lid of the crate. "Miss Andersen—she's in dog heaven. Surrounded by meat-on-the-bone and all those toys she done buried. Ain't that right, Miss Andersen?"

The idea of dog heaven had never entered Edie's mind, but she found the prospect surprisingly reassuring. So much more plausible, somehow, than an afterlife for humans. Yet it also had all the makings of a fairytale. While Sammy dug a grave beneath the wisteria arbor, laboring in determined silence, she reflected on the ease with which he spoke of a paradise of dog toys. As much as she loved stories, her talent was for cataloguing them, never creating them. She admired—even envied—those who could shape a fantasy out of inchoate nothing.

"Would it be alright if I say a psalm?" asked Sammy.

Edie nodded. She watched his lips move, but didn't absorb the words. After that, he filled the grave quickly.

"You'll get a new dog," said Sammy. "You'll feel much better."

"I hope dog heaven is a nice place," said Edie.

"You know it is," he answered. Then he patted her on the side of the shoulder, very hesitantly, as though touching a scalding object. "You take good care of yourself, Miss Crossgrove," he said. "I'll be seeing you in two weeks."

"But I owe you—"

"Not for today," he said. "I'm no undertaker."

.....

Each passing day brought more resolution to Edie's memories. She uncovered new ones too, like hidden markers at the corner of a cemetery: the morning Sammy had wished her a happy July Fourth, the occasion she'd seen him tuck a sprig of forsythia above his ear when he thought that nobody was watching. Daydreaming had never come easily to Edie—particularly after her parents' deaths, she hadn't allowed her thoughts to drift—but now she found her mind chasing every last wisp of fancy. Her writing fell by the wayside. Some days, she didn't bother to dress until the afternoon. Often she'd be seized with an idea—maybe that Sammy had left a glove in the mismatched clothing bin—and she'd dig through the mounds of socks and slippers in search of a traceable label. None of these efforts ever panned out, of course. Sammy hadn't left so much as a photograph or a footprint. One night, Edie woke in a dreadful panic, afraid she'd imagined him entirely. It took a lengthy inventory of her own memories to convince herself otherwise.

But so what? So Sammy had existed. The problem was that she had absolutely no claim on him—no recognized right to pursue him. They hadn't been friends, even implicitly, not like Jessica Tandy and Morgan Freeman in *Driving Miss Daisy*. And she hadn't been secretly in love with him like that butler character was with the housekeeper in *The Remains of the Day*. Most certainly not. Their relationship was far simpler than that: professional. Employer and employee. But not in the way Ray Kroc and the fry cooks at McDonalds were employer and employee. She wanted to tell people that he was the man who'd buried her dog, but that sounded absolutely nutty out-of-context. There was the problem with human relationships—you could never really explain them. Sammy had simply been Sammy. Why wasn't it enough of a claim on him that she cared what had happened to him? Obviously, it wasn't.

. . . . .

The second time Liz Blatch came over to complain about the state of Edie's yard, she brought along her husband. Ted Blatch was a short man with a long face. He traded currency on Wall

Street—but his bachelor's degree had been in chemical engineering, which somehow made him an authority on lawn care.

"I'm not a lawyer," he explained. "But I've done some extensive research and I know full well what I'm talking about."

"I'm sure you do," agreed Edie.

The last time Ted Blatch had been in her parlor, he'd explained to her the advantages of resurveying the property line. He'd wanted to split the costs. Before that, it had been an overhanging crabapple limb.

"This state has something called an attractive nuisance doctrine, Miss Crossgrove," said Blatch. "And what you've got out front—that pasture of yours—is unquestionably an attractive nuisance."

Edie surveyed the backs of her hands, wishing she might read the liver spots like tea leaves. "You know what that reminds me of?" she asked. "That scene in that picture, you know which one, where Marlon Brando explains the Napoleonic Code . . . to Vivien Leigh. . . . What was the name of that picture?"

Liz glanced pointedly at her husband. He cupped his fist in his palm.

"Please try to focus, Miss Crossgrove," he said. "Nobody's talking about Vivien Leigh."

"I thought *I* was," answered Edie. "I've got it. *On the Waterfront.*"

"You're not listening to me, Miss Crossgrove," insisted Blatch. "A homeowner has responsibilities. You've got to think about safety . . . and, to be honest, property values. . . . You've got no right to grow a forest on your lawn."

"What's wrong with a forest?" snapped Edie. "It was a forest before it was a lawn, wasn't it? And it's more natural this way—better for the environment."

"So you're just going to let it keep growing?" demanded Blatch.

"Until Sammy comes back," answered Edie. "Then, we'll see . . ."

"Please, Miss Crossgrove," interjected Liz. "This is an untenable situation. We're not the only other people on this block. Seymour Klein is going to come over here one day this week and mow the place himself."

"I warned him about the liability," added Ted. "But he doesn't care. He says he's an OB-GYN and he's had it up to here with liability..."

Edith removed her glasses and cleaned them on her quilt. "I wouldn't do that if I were Dr. Klein," she said. She didn't remember Klein ever moving in, but she was willing to concede his existence—for argument's sake. "That would be a grave error in judgment."

"But what other choice does he have.... Do we have?" asked Liz. "You're painting us into a corner. We're on your side, Miss Crossgrove..."

"Oh, there are *sides* now," said Edie. "Well Sammy's on my side and Sammy doesn't like strangers mucking about with his lawn."

"I guess that's his problem," said Blatch.

"He killed a man, you know," continued Edie. "About fifteen years ago, in North Carolina. He caught a fellow mowing one of his lawns—a Mexican, I think—and Sammy pumped him full of buckshot..."

"That's just awful," cried Liz. "A man like that has no business in East Salem. He should be in jail."

"He was. Nearly six months. But he was a World War II vet and the other guy was illegal, so they gave him a break.... In any case, I wouldn't go cutting one of Sammy's lawns without permission. He's very possessive, proprietary—like a coyote. It wouldn't surprise me if there weren't booby-traps in that grass, even landmines."

Edie enjoyed watching the color rise in Liz Blatch's bony face. Making up Sammy's life was like writing a fairytale. It was genuinely fun. Deep down, it also left her a bit uneasy—akin to lying about a death in the family—but who was to say that Sammy wouldn't kill the obstetrician if he ever caught him on Edie's lawn? After thirty-seven years, people developed attachments.

Ted Blatch stood up swiftly. "I don't like being threatened, Miss Crossgrove."

"I'm not threatening anyone," said Edie. "I'm just looking out for your safety . . . I'd hate to see someone injured over a few blades of grass."

"Come on, Liz," said Blatch. "We don't need to take this."

Liz rose reluctantly. "If you reconsider, Miss Crossgrove . . ."

"I have reconsidered."

"You have?"

"It wasn't *On the Waterfront*. Most certainly not. That wouldn't make any sense at all. It was *A Streetcar Named Desire*—The picture had to take place in Louisiana, dear, because that's the only state they have the Napoleonic Code."

Liz shook her head, as though reprimanding a child.

"Enough, honey," Ted said sharply. "She's doing this on purpose."

Edie also wanted the Blatches to depart. She looked up at Liz and asked: "Tell me something. How *is* Julio in the sack?"

That was the one advantage of growing old—it let you be nasty with impunity.

. . . . .

At first, Edie felt relief. But then an intense despair overtook her. She watched the Blatches retreating up the front walk—they were arguing something fierce now—and she was reminded of her own powerlessness. What could she do if this alleged obstetrician really did attempt to mow her lawn? She knew the answer to that question all too well: absolutely nothing. She might craft up any stories she wanted about Sammy, but talking didn't make it so. At the end of the day, she didn't have so much as a guard dog to protect her. Not that Hans Christian Andersen had been much of a guardian . . . but at least she'd had a powerful yelp. In the high grass, the obstetrician might have mistaken her for a pit-bull or a German Shepherd.

Edie laughed. That anybody could mistake her ridgeback for an attack dog! A retreat dog was more like it. But Sammy had been wrong about one thing—she'd never replaced the animal. If there really were a dog heaven, it might well be contiguous with human heaven, and Edie didn't like the idea of walking more than one dog at a time. So she was a one-dog woman—and that dog was in a crate under the arbor.

The crate! Where the idea came from, Edie didn't know—but it came. Hadn't the crate contained Bibles from Sammy's church? And possibly an address label? Under the circumstances, Hans Christian Andersen would forgive her.

Edie wheeled hard toward the side door, forgetting there was no lift at the entrance to the garage. Then she backtracked through the kitchen and into the sunlight. She hadn't been outside in months—not since she'd started having the groceries delivered—and she was shocked at how high the grass had grown. The hedgerows were creeping into the flowerbeds, and maple saplings had sprouted up willy-nilly. Beside the driveway, where the ridgeback was buried, the arbor had collapsed under the weight of the lilac and wisteria vines. Motoring across the undergrowth was like riding on horse-back over a mountain range. Twice, Edie nearly fell out of the chair. When she finally reached the gravesite, she realized that she didn't have a shovel. She had no choice but to lower herself to the ground and to burrow through the dirt by hand.

The earth gave way with surprising ease. It had rained the night before, leaving the soil soft and damp and cool. Crabgrass tickled Edie's ears, but she didn't bother to scratch them. All that mattered was finding that crate—before time and the elements might do any further damage. If only she could remember precisely where Sammy had lain the animal to rest...

Tears of frustration trickled down Edie's cheeks. She'd dug a long trough, and several craters—the arbor looked like it had been shelled by cannon—but she'd uncovered not so much as a splinter. Was it possible the box had decayed entirely—that other animals had scavenged the bones? And then she hit wood! A solid thump. Edie used a stone to scrape away the earth until the address on the crate was clearly visible, lacquered in transparent tape and preserved for the ages.

That's when the first paroxysm seized her. The numbness lay in her left side now, her good side. She couldn't move. She couldn't scream. She was lying on her front lawn, but the grass was far too high for anybody to see her. Edie thought all was without hope when she spotted Sammy, smiling, chugging over the rise on his mower. He was slashing the grass, plowing a path toward her rescue. But he was a young, robust Sammy, wearing sunglasses, whistling—mounted atop a shiny red chassis—and even as Edie reached out toward him, she saw that he wasn't coming any closer. Soon the distance between them started increasing, slowly at first, then faster, like a locomotive pulling away from the land of fairytales.

Hazardous Cargoes

Know your load.

That's rule *numero uno* in this business, which is why I make them count the penguins out in front of me one at a time. I'm not going to be the schmuck who shows up in Orlando two birds short of a dinner party. Or the screw-up who's got to explain to the highway patrol exactly how sixty kilos of coke ended up in his rig without his noticing. Short John Silver used to tell about one fellow who kept trying to turn his radio off, over and over again, but it just wouldn't shut off, and when he pulled into a rest stop for the night, he realized he'd got a ten-piece mariachi band camping out in his trailer. So I always insist on a comprehensive inventory. And the guys at the zoo grumble about it, giving me looks as icy as the day is hot, but they do it. So I know I'm pulling out of Houston with exactly forty-two Gentoo penguins, seventeen Jamaican land iguanas, four tuataras from New Zealand, and a pair of rare, civet-like mammals called linsangs. No more, no less.

Some drivers like to get themselves a five-course breakfast before they hit the road, but I'm one for hauling and *then* eating. It gives you a sense of accomplishment, knowing you've already covered so much ground. Besides, you avoid the pre-dawn crunch at Waffle House and Denny's: If you pull off the Interstate mid-morning, you're bound to be one of the only faces in the trucker's lounge. And you get better service at the counter too, maybe even an ear to yak at. My plan is to push as far as Lake Charles by noon, but it's sweltering, even with the A/C, so I pull into a Mister Bigbee's to fuel up my bloodstream and check on the penguins.

Alaxa is my waitress. She's tall and thin, maybe a bit flat-chested, with a tiny gray tuft above each ear, but not bad-looking except for a large, tear-shaped mole under her nose. I'm curious what kind of name Alaxa is—Guatemalan? Croat?—but I know that's a lousy way to strike up a conversation. Makes me sound like the Border Patrol. More toxic in this part of the country than asking her age or her weight. Instead, I order a chef's salad and tell her about the penguins.

"For real?" she asks.

Her accent is straight-up East Texas: like honey dripping from the hive. It strikes me that Alaxa could be one of those made-up names. That's a weird business, made-up names. Like there's not enough real ones to go around? But the woman didn't choose her own name, so that's about that. "Forty-two Gentoo penguins," I say. "I counted them myself. That's the Short John Silver method. Count everything."

"You mean Long John Silver?" she asks. "Like the restaurant?"

"*Short* John Silver. He was a good buddy of mine," I answer. But that's like saying Joe Stalin had a mean streak. What I want to say is that I've been missing Short John Silver like I lost my own dad. It's funny how you can see a guy only three, four times a year, and still he's close as family. Better than family. I've got a wife, and a son, and two brothers, and a whole slew of aunts and uncles and cousins, and I haven't seen any of them in a good five years. "He lost a leg to bone cancer as a kid. And never wore a prosthesis, just used a crutch. Like Long John Silver. But he was hardly five feet, so we called him *Short* John."

"Whatever works for you," says Alaxa. I realize she hasn't read *Treasure Island*.

"He took a spill in Natchez last winter," I say. "During that big ice storm. Nobody told him the drawbridge was jammed open."

Alaxa clears some pocket change from the adjacent table and drops it into the pouch of her apron. "Can I see them?" she asks.

"What?"

"Can I see the penguins?"

If I were looking for a hook-up, penguins would make excellent bait. But I'm not. At forty-two years old, what I want is a little peace and quiet—the reassurance of knowing that I'll find my personal belongings where I've left them. I deposit a rumpled ten dollar bill on the tabletop. "Sure thing," I say. Alaxa turns to the other waitress, a chunky girl with an oversized crimson bow in her hair, and announces she's going on break.

Outside, the air is toxic. A hot breeze ruffles the banner announcing "Free Coffee" between 5:30 and 7:00 am. Rainbows whirl in the oil puddles on the asphalt. Along the traffic median, a solitary crow picks at a discarded wrapper. I climb up onto the platform and undo the locks.

"Penguins," she says. "Strange thing to be driving around with."

"Penguins are nothing," I say. "My buddy, Short John Silver, back in the fifties, before the HAZMAT rules, he carried a nuclear warhead over the George Washington Bridge into New York City. Parked it right in front of the Chrysler Building while he ate lunch at an automat."

"For real?" asks Alaxa.

"For real."

There's two separate doors to the rig, one for the warm compartment, one for the cool compartment, the sections divided by some high-tech synthetic glass. I roll open the cool door and the frigid air blasts us. It's so cold it burns, like the opposite of a blow torch. The penguins appear pink under the coils of fluorescent light, their deep-orange bills protruding like mercury thermometers. They appear perpetually stunned. On the opposite side of the divider, the tuataras hiss in apparent displeasure. Alaxa extends a small, bony hand, and I hoist her onto the platform. I slide the door shut behind us, but only two-thirds of the way—to conserve cold without giving my companion any wrong impressions. If I have any goal in life, other than just minding my own business, it's to keep another waitress from hoodwinking me into marrying her.

"There was a movie about penguins," says Alaxa. "But I didn't see it."

"*March of the Penguins*," I say. "But those were Emperor penguins. These are Gentoos."

"They're cute," she says. "You've got a cool job."

"*I* think so," I answer.

I make a point of counting the birds again before I pull out of the lot. How a truck-stop waitress could make off with a rare penguin, or why, I couldn't tell you, but people do things like that, so it can't hurt to be too careful.

.....

From Lake Charles to Baton Rouge, I'm listening to Orson Welles read *Tess of the D'Urbervilles*. There's another habit I acquired from Short John: Literature. The very first day he picked me up—a sixteen year old runaway out of Southwest Florida—he had a tape deck playing *The Grapes of Wrath*. That was in the days before you could buy audio novels. What Short John did was have his girls record the novels for him while he was on the road. He'd pull into Amarillo, crash a few days with this teacher's aide named Bonnie Lou, come away with seven volumes of Proust in ninety minute segments. He had funny-looking girlfriends all over the map making tapes for him—plain-Jane country gals reading James Joyce in hayseed voices. It was practically a goddam cottage industry. He'd adapted the idea from his grandfather, who used to work for the cigar roller's union, which hired professional readers to educate the men while they labored. Lots of fellows think I'm nuts for listening to audio books—like CEO's who knit, or football players who do ballet in their spare time. But at the end of the day, I know something about something, and most drivers don't know jack squat.

So I'm rooting for Tess. I know things aren't going to work out for her—I've heard this novel at least half a dozen times—but I'm doing what Short John used to call "suspending my disbelief," when it crosses my mind to check what year Welles recorded these tapes. Idle curiosity. Luckily, I've still got the original hard plastic package. "Copyright 1980." Same year my Mom died, and I left Fort Myers. Long time ago. Indifferently, I toss the package into the back of the cab. What comes back at me is a startled yelp. High-pitched and sudden. I glance at the rearview mirror as I edge to the side of the Interstate. There's a threadbare beach blanket behind my seat, and it's trying not to move, but giving itself away with tiny, lapping breaths. It's keeping too still for anything *un*-human. I ease my utility knife out from beside the ashtray. Once we've crossed the rumble strip, I shift into neutral. Then I yank hard on a corner of the blanket. The cloth gives quickly at first, but abruptly it starts tugging back.

"Let go," I say. "*Now*. Unless you want to get shot."

After a long pause, the tension lets up. When I draw back the blanket, I'm staring down at a blinking teenager. My stowaway has a shaved head and a chin-stud. It takes me several seconds to register that she's a girl. A square-jawed, not-so-pretty girl wearing camouflage pants and a white tank-top, sporting a duffle bag with a skull-and-crossbones markered into the canvas. Tess of the D'Urbervilles, she isn't. If it weren't for the well-developed contents of her sweat-soaked tank-top—and how can I help noticing—my stowaway could probably pass as a child.

The girl scrutinizes me carefully, as though deciding whether she can take me in a scuffle. "Where's your gun?" she asks.

I feel self-conscious holding a knife on a teenage girl. But you never know if she's got a canister of mace in her pants. I keep the blade low, not wanting to attract the attention of passing motorists.

"This isn't a taxicab," I say. "Stowing away is stealing. It's theft of services. No different than taking money out of a cash register."

My passenger frowns, pursing her large lips. The stench of sewage rises from a nearby drainage ditch and drifts in through the open window. Each passing rig generates a gust of hot, angry wind.

"As soon as we get to Richmond, I'll get out," she says. "Don't be a jerk. It's not going to cost you anything."

"I'm not going to Richmond. I'm going to Orlando."

"But the address on the truck says Richmond."

"Like I said, I'm going to Orlando," I say. I could explain how I'm only a contract driver—penguins one day, cruise missiles the next—and that the company that leases the trucks for delivering zoo animals is based in Virginia, but that's the kind of conversation that invites complications. "I'll take you as far as Baton Rouge," I say. "But that's the end of the line."

"Okay," the girl says. "I thought you were going to Richmond."

I pull back onto the highway. While we've been negotiating, something drastic has happened between Tess and Alec D'Urberville. I've heard this story God knows how many times, but I can't remember exactly what. So I rewind the tape. "You can sit up front, if you want to . . ." I say.

"I'm fine here," she says. "My grandmother lives in Richmond. Say, do you know any other truck drivers going to Richmond?"

At least she's trying to get someplace, I think. Someplace *specific*. When Short John picked me up, I just wanted to get as far away from my step-father as possible. Wasn't anything *wrong* with my step-father, either. Just wasn't anything right with him. Kind of man spends his entire life collecting SSI and eating cheese doodles in front of a television with piss-poor reception. So I'm glad my stowaway has a grandmother in Richmond. What I don't like is having her behind me, where I can't see her.

"What's your name?" I ask.

The girl says nothing. I give her a long time to think. She takes a cigarette out of her bag, and twirls it between her fingers, but knows better than to light it. Obviously, she's a middle-class kid—the kind of daughter some family is going to be searching for—and that leaves me uneasy.

"Can't you help me hitch a ride to Richmond?" she says. "Don't be a jerk."

"This isn't a travel agency," I say. "How old are you?"

"Old enough."

"Old enough to get raped and murdered by a crazy motherfucker truck driver you don't know from Adam? Ever thought about that?"

"Just take me to Baton Rouge, okay?" she says. That's a conversation stopper, if ever there was one. I flip the tape back on. I'm just starting to lose myself in *Tess*, to forget I've got company, when she adds, "Old enough to say some crazy motherfucker truck driver did stuff to her without her wanting it. Ever thought about *that*?"

You bet I've thought about that. That's why I'm not leaving her on the side of I-10. But I don't want to get picked up for aiding and abetting, either. Who knows why she's leaving Houston and who's after her?

"Baton Rouge," I say.

She shuffles forward, resting her chin on the seatback. "And can we listen to something else on the radio? This shit is giving me a headache."

"Tell me your name and I'll think about it."

"Viktoria," she says. "With a K."

"Well, Viktoria with a K," I say. "I've thought about it. . . . This is *my* truck. And this *shit* is *Tess of the D'Urbervilles* by Thomas Hardy. Which is what we're going to listen to, all the way to Baton Rouge. And if for some reason we do get to the end of the whole goddam novel, then we're going to start over again at the very beginning. Am I making myself clear?"

"Clear as crystal," she says. "Just one question for you."

"Yeah?"

"Is it really your truck? Or do you just drive it?"

"Shut up," I say. "Try and learn something."

. . . . .

We're on the outskirts of Lafayette, Louisiana, when Viktoria "with a K" announces that she wants to use the ladies' room. If she was a boy, I'd just send her out to the side of the road and let her water the tule grass. But with a girl, even a tomboy with an attitude, I recognize that really would make me into a jerk. So I've got two crummy choices: Either I dispatch her into a rest stop alone, and hope she doesn't say something that gets me hauled off to Leavenworth, or I find a place for us both to take a breather together. As much as I don't like the idea of walking into a luncheonette with somebody else's teenage daughter, or losing the hour, a guy has got to play the cards he's been dealt. Keeping my passenger on a tight leash seems like the surest route to getting my penguins to Orlando by the end of the week.

We pull up at a restaurant called Doctor Bigger's. Clearly a play on Mister Bigbee's, though right now they're pitching a "health-conscious menu" with low-carb soups and a "king-size" salad bar. But it's a sham, if you ask me. Nobody loses weight eating anyplace with laminated menus. The dining room is pretty full—maybe because outside it's ninety-seven degrees and in here it's like a meat locker—so the waitress seats us in the back section, the smoking-section, opposite a slot machine. "Special soup today is cream of barley," she says. "Free refills on the iced tea." She's about my age, maybe a few years younger. Flaming orange hair. Clearly natural. Big brown eyes under dark blue eyeliner. Sadly, she doesn't have a nametag. When Viktoria shuffles off to the restroom, the waitress stares after her.

"It's a rough age," she says.

"She's not my daughter," I answer. Regretting it the moment I say it.

The waitress's face loses some of its friendliness. But only some. "She your niece?" she asks.

"Friend of the family," I say. "I'm taking her over to her grandmother's."

That seems to satisfy her. She shrugs. "Rough age," she says. When she comes back to take our order, she's all smiles again.

I tell Viktoria to go first. She insists she isn't hungry.

"We've got a long drive ahead of us," I say. But not wanting to draw too much suspicion, I add quickly, "More than an hour to Baton Rouge."

The girl pushes the menu away. "I'm old enough to decide when I'm hungry."

"Why do we have to go through this *every time* we visit your grandmother?" I say. I roll my eyes at the waitress, hoping for sympathy. "Your grandmother gave me more than enough money to pay for you."

Viktoria picks up my cue. Maybe a bit too clearly. Once it's established I'm paying, she orders enough food to feed half of Africa for a week. Sides of fries and onion rings, an okra appetizer, two breakfast entrees. For dessert: A chocolate milkshake *and* a banana split. I throw her a dirty look, but there's not much else I can do. When the waitress leaves, she says, "Chill out. Grandma can afford it."

She's beaming. She thinks this "grandma" routine is funny.

"Lend me a quarter," she says. "I want to play some music."

I do as I'm told. Soon, a high-pitched, pulsing noise rises out of the tableside jukebox. It has corresponding lyrics, totally indecipherable. Apparently, this is music. I suddenly feel ancient as the pyramids of Egypt: To this girl, the Rolling Stones, and the Beatles, and goddam Frank Sinatra, are more or less the same thing. I can't help wondering if my own son listens to this stuff—but I don't wonder too hard. Ever since Maureen won full custody, I don't let myself go there.

"I started driving rigs when I was sixteen," I tell Viktoria. "Friend named Short John Silver set me up with a buddy of his who delivered carpets. Told them I was twenty-one and had a commercial license." I did have a commercial license too—bought for fifteen bucks in the French Quarter. "You can't get away with that anymore. On account of the terrorism crackdown."

"Tell me later," she says. "You're wasting the song."

So I sit with my hands on the paper placemat until the food comes. After that, I watch Viktoria eat. She wolfs down three scrambled eggs and four slices of French toast, then starts in on the ice cream. One damn hungry kid. Myself, I don't have much of an appetite. At the next booth, there's a trucker and his girl. I can tell he's a trucker because he's wearing a plaid hunting jacket. Only a trucker thinks to bring a jacket with him to a restaurant on a hot summer day. Or maybe an off-duty firefighter.

"What are you running away from?" I ask.

She slurps her shake loudly through a straw. She's drinking a milkshake and smoking a cigarette at the same time. "People like you," she says.

"Thanks."

"You got penguins in your truck," she says. "I heard you talking to that chick after breakfast."

"Maybe."

"Will you let me see them? I've never seen a live penguin before."

Now I know how to make it as a pedophile. Forget lollypops. Antarctic wildlife is the ticket. I try again. "What are you running away from?"

"Stuff. Bad stuff," she says. "Please, can I see the penguins?"

"We'll see. Maybe once we get to Baton Rouge," I say. "Can't go disturbing them every time somebody wants to be amused."

At that moment, our nameless waitress reemerges from the kitchen, the swinging doors slapping to and fro in her wake. She slides the bill face-down onto the table. Then she turns to Viktoria, as though I'm not even there, and asks: "You okay, sugar?"

The girl looks me over. I can see the newfound power in her eyes.

I mouth the word penguins, probably too conspicuously.

"I'm fine," she says. Decisively. "Why? Was Dad giving you a hard time?"

My sudden paternity catches the waitress off guard. She must sense this is a situation well above her pay grade, because that's the last we ever see of her. A bald man with a walrus mustache rings us up at the counter.

On the way out, Viktoria insists I buy her a gumball. While she's waiting for the ball to swivel through a maze of grooves, building momentum to the bottom of a long, clear chute, the guy from the next table comes up to me. He's taken off his jacket and he's got his hands in the pockets of his jeans. "Saw you've got live cargo," he says.

I watch Viktoria retrieve the gumball. "Penguins," I say. "Forty-two of them."

"You headed east or west?"

"East," I say. "Probably."

"Keep a heads-up," he says. "Potholes like crazy, about two miles this side of Crowley."

"That so?" I say. Non-committal. "Thanks."

"Holes the size of basketballs, man," he says. More emphatically. "Crater-of-the-fucking moon."

"I'll keep a lookout," I say.

"Just wanted to give you a heads-up," he says again. "Wouldn't want to see you jackknife with a load of penguins."

But he would, of course. That's human nature. Nothing more basic than wanting to see another guy's penguins flailing around in a ditch.

.....

By the time we're at the turnoff for Jennings, I've given up on Tess and her D'Urberville aspirations. Viktoria has started in on seeing the penguins again, and she won't let Orson Welles get a word in edgewise. "You showed them to that chick back in Lake Charles," she says peevishly. "You just wanted to get laid, didn't you?"

This doesn't deserve an answer. I take a deep breath and let it pass.

Viktoria snaps off the tape player. "How long since you've been laid, mister?"

We're thrusting through the belly of the swamp. The highway's an elevated track between towering cypresses. Lots of road-kill:

mule deer, ring-tailed raccoons, other furry carcasses mutilated beyond recognition. Also an occasional live armadillo, waddling at the base of a grassy embankment. Not a promising place to abandon an teenager from the big city. But I'm sorely tempted.

"Bet it's been a long time," says the girl. "Bet I'm the closest thing you've had to a date in ages."

That's too much. "Mind your own fucking business," I say.

"What language!" she gasps, all mock-southern-belle, but totally absurd coming from a girl wearing dog-tags around her neck. "Someone must have hit an open sore."

I turn to face her, keeping one eye on the road. I try to look as unruffled as possible. "You ready to tell me why you're running away?"

"I told you. Bad stuff," she says. "What do you care?"

I shrug. "Maybe I *don't* care."

That's all I say. I know this is a game that I can win. At my age, I'm willing to wait an awfully long time to get what I want. We pass the turnoffs for Estherwood, for Forked Island, for Hominy Heights. Not a peep from my passenger. But two miles out of Crowley, just past the bend where the highway narrows down to three lanes, she says, "I don't get along with my dad, okay? Can we leave it at that?"

"But you get along with your grandmother?" I say.

"Yeah," she says. Nothing more.

"I had a stepfather I didn't get along with," I say.

She folds her arms across her chest. "Good for you."

I want to make eye contact with her, but she's staring straight ahead. Practically boring holes into the windshield. A bright-red SUV passes us on the right. "Why don't you get along with him?" I ask.

"Look, I told you why I'm leaving. Now, can I see the fucking penguins?"

"Don't change the subject," I say. "We were talking about your dad."

She turns and glares at me. "What does a girl have to do around here to see a few fucking penguins? I didn't know it was such a big deal, all of a sudden. It wasn't when you were trying to screw that waitress. Why don't I just give you a hand-job and then you show me the penguins and we'll call it even?"

"Viktoria—"

"Or how about if you don't show me the fucking penguins, I'll run into the next gas station we pass and tell them I gave you a hand-job."

Her voices is breaking—she's on the verge of tears—but I'm too agitated to care.

"You want penguins, dammit," I shout. "I'll show you penguins."

I shift into a lower gear, intending to pull to the rig onto the shoulder. But I've still got my hand on the transmission when we hit a pothole the size of Rhode Island. That guy in the restaurant wasn't kidding about the craters of the moon. One pothole is not going to knock out a rig, of course. It's the next three—one after another, like artillery shells—that whack the axles out from under us. Before I can say so-long-sweet-Jesus, glass is shattering in my ears. Then I'm wedged sideways as the cab lands horizontal to the roadbed. I can actually see the wheels of the trailer spinning through the passenger-side window.

All of my limbs seem to move. I feel the trickle of blood over my temple, but I know not to reach for it. If there's a hole in my brain, no need to poke a finger in it. If it's just something superficial, no need to get my hands bloody.

"Holy fuck," says the girl.

"You okay?" I ask.

"You could have fucking killed us," she says. I guess that means she's all right.

I throw my shoulder against the door of the cab. It inches open with a painful, scraping sound. I scoot across the hot metal and then I help clamber Viktoria out after me. Luckily, we're the only overturned vehicle. No other crushed cars. That's a driver's worst nightmare: somebody else's baby pinned to death under your rig. But this is a textbook one-party wreck. In front of us, the highway stretches through the swampland. Open and empty. A few cars slow down for an instant, then plow forward. Behind us, the road is totally impassible. Traffic is building up quickly.

The wound in the side of the truck is large enough to drive a Cadillac through. The siding has peeled away like the lid of a sardine can. Both generators have conked out in the cooler of the truck, so the A/C's off, but glacial air is rising as steam from the gash in the siding. We're basically trying to refrigerate the entire bayou. "Get back," I warn Viktoria. "Now! Whole goddam thing could go up." Then I climb into the damaged trailer and gather up a handful of penguins.

I run them across the highway to Viktoria, in twos and three, like a one-man bucket brigade. Their tiny bodies feel warm and dry, not soft and slick, to the touch. But they flail a lot. Who can blame them? A middle-aged Indian woman has gotten out of her car and is helping the girl look after the birds. The good Samaritan is wearing some kind of traditional robe, with gold trim, that must be hell in this weather. "Try to keep the birds off the hot asphalt," I shout. And then I'm back again with another pair of Gentoos.

More people are piling out of vehicles. One big black guy identifies himself as a medical student. He wants to take a look at my forehead. I hand him an unconscious linsang. Out-cold, but breathing.

"Does this thing bite?" he asks.

"How the hell should I know?" I answer.

Someone else shouts: "Look! Penguins!"

In the end, the tuataras are all dead. Crushed by the rear axle going through the flooring. But I've rescued both linsangs and all the iguanas, not to mention forty-one penguins. The forty-second has gone AWOL. That's truly priceless. An AWOL penguin. Like something out of a comic strip.

"How long can these things last in this heat?" asks Viktoria.

The answer, I know, is *not long enough*.

I've always been one to avoid cops, but now I need one more than Jesus Christ needs a nail remover. Unfortunately, I don't hear so much as a siren. Only horns honking, shouts. But I do catch sight of a box-truck a few rows back in traffic. It looks like the refrigerated sort. Has "Oscar's Originals" in calligraphy on the paneling. I wade between cars and signal for the driver to roll down his window. "What you got in there?"

"Meat," he says. He has an open, weasel-like face and bad acne scars around his mouth. "Kosher-style meat."

I rub my tongue over my front teeth. "I got penguins," I say.

"You got shit luck," he says.

"That too. Penguins need to be kept cool. How'd you like to sell all that meat to the Orlando Zoo at cost, and let me refrigerate some penguins."

"I'd like to help you, guy," he says. Nervous. "But you know how it is . . ."

"No, I don't know how it is. You see: These penguins here are endangered species. Only a few left in the world." I'm pulling this shit out of my ass, right and left. But I figure: What's this fellow going to know about penguins? "Think about it. There's going to be television crews out here in a few minutes. Do you want to be the guy who's face gets flashed all over the Internet because he wouldn't sacrifice a few pounds of sirloin for forty-one endangered penguins? Or do you want to be the guy with his picture in the paper for saving them?"

"They're that rare, are they?"

"Very rare," I say. "Not what's your plan? Because if you're not playing ball, I'm going to go find another truck."

The guy opens his cab door and steps down. "Okay, do it. But they better pay for the whole load. Market value."

I'm already headed back to retrieve my first batch of penguins. "Walt Disney funds the zoo, for Christ's sake," I call after him. "They're richer than God."

The guy with the meat shipment manages to pull his truck forward fifty yards. Other motorists let him past grudgingly. In under five minutes, we've loaded the birds into the truck and handed out free cold-cuts to anyone who'll take them.

"Forty-one for forty-two isn't bad," I say. To nobody in particular. But then the last of the penguins comes shuffling out from behind a mangrove hedge. How the hell it got there, I'll never know. But it's the missing bird—there's no doubt about that. When its webbed feet touch the scorching pavement, the creature begins to wobble in confusion, or maybe pain, and it topples over onto its wing. I scoop the bird up in my arms and cradle it like an infant.

That's when the first squad car appears. Two state troopers. One an Asian officer in reflective sunglasses. Built like a linebacker. The other a tall white guy with a blotchy complexion. But both cops—a common denominator that trumps race and religion and just about everything else. Cops are cops. These two park diagonally across the highway, like they own it, between my rig and the stopped traffic. Meanwhile, I attempt to soothe the penguin with a lullaby. *Rock-a-bye-birdie, on the tree top*... I sway my torso while I sing. I have every right to be carrying this penguin, I know, but I feel like I've stolen a chicken.

"This your truck?" asks the Asian cop.

"Yes, officer."

Viktoria approaches and I hand her the final bird.

"What's that?" asks the cop.

"It's a penguin," I say. "I got a whole truck of them."

The other cop whistles. "Penguins. This just takes the shit."

Viktoria is holding the penguin's face up to her own. "I think this one's injured."

"Who's she?" asks the first cop.

I look from Viktoria to the penguin and back to Viktoria. They both appear so damn helpless, so out of place.

"That's my daughter," I say. "We're on our way to Orlando, Florida."

The cop nods. My relationship with Viktoria doesn't interest him. "So you're carrying penguins?" he asks.

"Forty-two penguins, seventeen land iguanas, four tuataras and a pair of linsangs," I say. "But the tuataras are all dead."

While I spell "tuatara" and "linsang" for the cop, more police cars arrive on the scene. One of the new cops, a detective in a jacket and tie, asks me if a tuatara is some kind of a weapon. I overhear another of the cops tell Viktoria: "You'll have to leave those birds alone, miss. They're evidence." What a goddam mess! No matter how hard you try to mind your own business, eventually, no matter what precautions you take, you're bound to find yourself surrounded by a bunch of flailing penguins.

I walk a few yards up the roadbed and phone my outfitters in Richmond. They're not thrilled, obviously, but they're insured up the wazoo. Wrecks are just the cost of doing business. Once I work things out with them, they give Orlando a heads-up and make the arrangements for a relief vehicle. With penguins, you might think there'd be more of a fuss. And there is for the media, but not for the shippers. At the end of the day, the protocol is the same for Gentoo penguins, and soybeans, and sheets of aluminum siding. Cargo is cargo. It's when a guy gets too attached to his cargo—when he starts thinking of them as *his* penguins—that he gets himself into trouble.

I find Viktoria behind one of the squad cars. She's arm wrestling with a female state trooper. Losing every time. When she sees me, the girl grins. The female trooper bends Viktoria's slender arm to the trunk of the vehicle. Then she pats my daughter on the shoulder and wanders off.

"Hi, Dad," says Viktoria. "Look, I'm sorry about before. In the truck."

"You should be sorry," I say. But I put my hand on the scruff of her bare neck, like an uncle might, and I say: "I spoke to my boss. They're going to send a new truck from Shreveport. It should be here in a couple of hours."

"And you're taking me all the way to Florida?" she asks. Expectant.

"It looks like I am," I say. "And then I'm getting an Atlantic Coast gig and driving you straight to your grandmother's in Richmond."

She nods, but she looks disappointed. Like she hoped I was going to adopt her or something. Take her under my wing. But I don't have that in me. I'm no *Short* John Silver. I have a kid of my own who I haven't spoken to in five years, who I should go track down sooner rather than later.

"Richmond," I say for emphasis. "The end of the line."

You've got to know your load. And you've got to know how far to carry it.

The Vermin Episode

We'd heard rumors of the difficulties that had befallen our neighbors, the Samsas, but we'd certainly never expected to become embroiled in their misfortune. In the five years that they occupied the flat opposite ours on Charlotte Street, while their familial habits offered us no grounds for complaint, they had held themselves conspicuously aloof from the leaseholders' meetings and the May Day festivities that composed the life of our building. My wife, Ryba, who also happened to be a distant cousin of Marjeta Samsa, and who had attended the *Beis Yakov* School for Girls with her when she was still Marjeta Berg, insisted that Josef Samsa was a closeted anti-Semite whose ineffable politeness masked deep shame at his wife's origins. In hindsight, I suspect the man was merely ashamed of his own commercial failings, which had taken his family from a seventeenth century mansion within shouting distance of Prague Castle to a four-room flat on the outskirts of the city. Whatever the causes of the Samsa family's reserve, the result was that we had little reason to interact with them until their adult son was transformed into a monstrous vermin. Even then, if the son had maintained his health, I suppose we'd have kept our distance and allowed the ill-fated Samsas to keep theirs. But when Gregor died, I insisted—over Ryba's objections—that we pay a condolence call, as we always do when a death occurs in the block. Why should it matter to the sight of an all-merciful God that the deceased had become a Gentile and a dung-beetle? As a rabbi, one must set an example.

Being uncertain when the Samsas would be home for visitors, as Marjeta had raised her children in the Catholic faith and could not be expected to sit seven nights of *shiva*, I dispatched the day maid, Lida Rikena, upstairs to their flat to inquire if we might pay our respects, and she was told we would be welcome that very evening at eight o'clock. Ryba and I then spent the better part of the noon hour discussing whether the occasion called for an offering of confections or pastry to sweeten the lives of the mourners, seeing as neither the traditions of the *halakha* nor common sense has much to say about grieving over enormous insects, and we finally settled upon a tasteful plate of cold prune *kolaches*. Or rather, *I* settled upon a plate of cold prune *kolaches* from the bakeshop in Jan Hus Square, and Ryba shook her head indignantly. At precisely eight o'clock, as the carillon peeled above St. Adalbert's, we climbed the three wooden flights from the ground floor to the Samsas' landing. From within the apartment rose a desperate, nearly inhuman wailing—a lament of Biblical intensity.

"I do hope another of them hasn't turned into a vermin," said Ryba. "You don't think it's catching, do you?"

"They're mourning," I said. "*Please*, doll."

"All the same," my wife answered, hugging my arm. "You can't be too careful."

We did not have time to confer any further, because at that moment the daughter, Grete, opened the door herself and invited us inside. She was a big-eyed, buxom young woman, far fairer than her mother, but she wore a dazed expression of the sort one sees on the survivors of streetcar accidents and young husbands who have lost their wives in childbirth. "I do apologize for keeping you in the cold," she said—in German, not Czech. "The servant girl gave her notice earlier this morning."

She led us down a narrow foyer into a spacious, well-lit parlor. We found the elder Samsas seated in adjacent high-backed chairs: Josef done up in his bank messenger's uniform, Marjeta bundled into a rather frumpy housedress and a black crepe bonnet. Nobody had made any effort to drape the mirrors or to stop the mantel clock, but at the center of the room stood an enormous plywood crate labeled: PRESERVED MEATS. In my mind, I had anticipated other guests—I had understood the son to be well-connected in the hosiery trade—and so a part of me regretted subjecting my dearest Ryba to this intimate encounter with her former classmate. When Josef rose to greet us, I handed him the box of *kolaches* and expressed my sincerest condolences. My wife pecked Marjeta on the cheek. That was all it took to send the woman into another fit of convulsive sobs.

"Let us be strong, Mama," said the daughter. She held her mother's head to her chest and gently patted the distraught woman's shoulders. "Gregor would have *wanted* us to be strong."

My wife took her cousin's knobby hand and squeezed it—an act that seemed quite natural, unless one understood how much this cost my Ryba. "You'll get through this," she said generously. "We're all here to *help* you get through this."

"You don't understand," cried Marjeta. "It's not your fault, Ryba. You don't have any children. If you'd had children of your own, then you'd understand..."

My wife's back stiffened as though—heaven forbid—she had been struck with a sudden bout of the polio. She glared at me, her jaw tight-set, her nostrils flaring, and I mouthed to her the words, "I love you," which was true. In the course of visiting sickbeds and shut-ins, a rabbi's wife must endure an excessive share of slights, and on occasions such as this one, Ryba's dignity and forbearance reminded me that I had chosen the right bride.

"We've had a most trying day," said Josef Samsa. "Most trying."

He patted the seat of an upholstered chair beside his own—a gesture well-suited for attracting a spaniel or a toddler—but I understood that he wished for me to sit down, so I did. The chair squealed under my modest weight and I could feel the iron springs poking into my buttocks.

Samsa leaned toward me and lowered his voice. "The truth of the matter, Herr Zeitz, is that we were hoping you might help us."

"Papa," interjected the daughter. "I'm sure the rabbi and his wife don't want to hear of our troubles."

"What choice do we have?" demanded Samsa. He threw his daughter a look of pained frustration—almost a plea for forgiveness—and then he continued. "I trust that by now, Herr Zeitz, you are aware of my family's difficulties," he said. "The peculiar difficulties preceding the death of my son, Gregor."

I nodded. Marjeta sobbed into her handkerchief.

"Then you must understand the additional burdens that we now face with regard to my son's remains," explained Samsa. "The cook had promised us that she would tend to arrangements, but I soon discovered that she'd packed the body in sawdust, and had the grocer's messenger haul it downstairs to the curbside for the rubbish men—which, even if *I* had been willing to accept this painful fate for my son, is not an end that his mother can tolerate."

"Assuredly not," I agreed. "Family is family, regardless of circumstances."

That was the moment I realized that the dead man's corpse lay inside the meat crate.

"Unfortunately, Father Cerny won't allow Gregor to be buried at Saint Ludmila's. He says that any man who suffers such a singular misfortune must be heavily yoked with sin—even if the precise nature of that sin remains unclear. I am afraid that the priest is not to be reasoned with on the subject," said Samsa, fingering his beard. "So I was hoping that, as a rabbi, you might find space for our son at the Jewish cemetery."

I will readily admit that I was caught off my guard by this request. It is not very often that I find myself asked to dispose of a colossal vermin's cadaver. Yet the boy had been born Jewish. Indeed, there was no questioning his matrilineal descent. And the burial of the dead is an obligation not to be trifled with—no matter how inconvenient it may prove.

I did not dare look at Ryba, who had cleared her throat audibly during the silence that followed Samsa's request, but I could sense her gaze boring into my flesh like two sharp, angry beams of sunlight. Instead, I focused on Josef Samsa, who had quickly diverted his own dark, depleted eyes toward the floorboards.

"Please help us," said Samsa—his voice barely audible. "We are desperate."

Watching this once proud man—a former member of the stock exchange—debase himself in front of his wife and daughter reminded me that I had no choice.

"I will do what I can," I offered.

I rose immediately and shook Samsa's hand.

"You'll send someone for the body?" he asked.

I found this request remarkably pushy, but a man cannot bestow half a gift.

"Very well. I'll send my nephews tomorrow before breakfast," I agreed. Then a flicker of concern passed through my mind. "On which side of the box are the feet located?"

Samsa appeared perplexed. "Honestly, I can't say. There were *so many feet*, you understand, poking in all directions." He toyed with his silver watch chain, training his eyes on the legs of his chair. "Do you know about the feet, Grete?"

"The cook did the packing," said Grete.

"Please make certain you look within that crate and mark the side containing the feet before my nephews arrive," I insisted. I was relieved to be assuming control of the situation again, although I still had not made eye contact with my wife. "I will not be having Damek and Karel carry a corpse head-first into the stairwell—and inviting half the neighborhood to follow the departed into the hereafter."

Then I shook Josef Samsa's hand and we took our leave quickly, before Ryba's kinsfolk had an opportunity to impose upon us any further.

.....

My wife did not speak in the hallway. Once we were safely ensconced within the warm and secure confines of our own flat, she stormed into the kitchen and slammed the iron teapot onto the gas range. Her hands trembled as she ignited the safety match.

"Please don't be angry, doll," I pleaded.

"I'm not angry," snapped Ryba. "I'm too upset to be angry."

"I'm sorry I put you through that," I said. "You've done a generous *mitzvah*."

I tried to wrap my arms around her waist from behind, but she shook herself loose.

"Did you hear that woman? She *still* thinks she's better than me." Ryba turned to face me and her eyes swelled with tears. "She thinks that because some rich *goy* took a fancy to her thirty years ago, she can trample all over me."

"He's not rich anymore."

"Tell *her* that."

"I don't need to tell her that. It's true. And I'm sure she already knows," I said. "Now would you rather be married to a rich *goy* or a dashingly handsome Jew?"

I knew this question would force a smile from Ryba, in spite of herself. She reached toward me and let me embrace her. Her hair—still its original chestnut hue—smelled wondrously of almond-scented perfume.

"Did you really have to offer to help them bury that thing?" she asked.

"It's not a *thing*, doll," I answered. "And yes, unfortunately, I did."

"Very well. I just hope you know what you've gotten us into," said Ryba. "A giant vermin isn't something that one disposes of every day."

With God's help, I thought—but I didn't say it. The Lord had transformed the dead man into a monstrous vermin, after all, and the fear crept into my heart that by assisting with his burial, I might not be furthering the divine plan, but rather standing in its way.

. . . . .

The next morning, as soon as we had concluded the *shacharit* prayers, I set out from the synagogue to the New Cemetery on foot, to speak directly with the chairman of the *chevra kadisha*. Yitzak Offener had taught natural sciences at the University for many years before retiring to administer the burial society, and I had always found him both honest and reasonable. While he certainly performed his duties most scrupulously—I have no doubt that every corpse interred under his watch had been appropriately cleansed and adorned—he was not above glancing the other way to permit the burial of a passing traveler, even if the deceased's origins and righteousness could not be unequivocally established. So traversing the Strasnice District and passing through the ivy-coated Renaissance gates of the burial ground, I clung to the hope that Offener and I might reach an understanding regarding the Samsa boy.

I had crossed the city quickly, braced by the crisp autumn air, and it was only half past seven when I arrived at my destination. Not wishing to accost Herr Offener before he had had an opportunity to savor his morning newspaper, I ventured into the oldest section of the cemetery to place stones atop the graves of my wife's parents. Then I paused at the open patch of earth beside my brother's monument, where Ryba and I had plans to rest. Gazing out at the sea of departed Pollaks and Zeitzes and Smolkovas, I found myself wondering what that poor salesman, Gregor Samsa, had done to earn his misfortune. Had he truly sinned in some unspeakable, unpardonable manner? Or had he simply been in the wrong place at the wrong time, like Susannah falsely accused by the Elders? And how does a person reconcile his faith in a benevolent God with the bald fact of a grown man turned into a dead bug? All I knew for certain was that I was now in possession of that grown man's earthly shards—my nephews had delivered them at dawn—and that I had a responsibility to see them tended to properly.

I followed the slate paths to Offener's headquarters, a small stone cabin tucked into the farthest corner of the cemetery. An unfamiliar clerk instructed me to wait on a long wooden bench in the antechamber, but seconds later, the chairman of the *chevra kadisha* ushered me into his busy office without delay. A conspicuous cloth bandage was wrapped around his forehead and tucked under his hat, but he did not appear to be in pain.

"You're all right?" I asked.

"An old war wound," Offener explained, grinning. "I went to war with the underside of the medicine chest in the washroom and it appears to have gotten the better of me." He adjusted the bandage and scratched beneath it with the tail of his fountain pen. "A few more soldiers like me would be the downfall of the Empire, I suppose. . . . And may I ask what brings Rabbi Zeitz all the way to Strasnice on a weekday morning?"

"A *mitzvah* for the both of us."

"That makes me nervous," answered Offener. "Your *mitzvahs* have a way about them."

I took a deep breath. "You are familiar with the Samsa boy?"

That was as far as I got before my host held up his hand. The casual cheer had melted rapidly from his features, replaced with a marble frown. "It cannot be done," he said.

"Please hear me out, Yitzhak," I persisted. "The mother is my wife's cousin. Don't you imagine we could find an out-of-the-way spot for him? Someplace where he might go unnoticed? As a personal favor, I'm asking you . . ."

"*I* would notice," answered Offener. "*God* would notice."

"Then what is to be done?" I demanded—trying to keep my frustration in check. I rose from my chair, bracing my palms against the mahogany desktop. "It is the body of a Jew. A *human being*. One can't just leave it at the curbside for the rubbish men to haul away."

The chairman of the *chevra kadisha* nodded sympathetically. "I'm not disagreeing with you," he said. "In the eyes of God, you may well be correct. But I'm not a rabbi, Jakub. I manage a cemetery. If I let you bury that thing here, there are many people who will feel that I have done something unholy—that I have polluted the ground where they've entrusted me to look after their loved ones." Offener scratched his wounded head more aggressively. "It's not a matter of looking the other way, I'm afraid. It simply *cannot* be done."

"Very well," I said curtly. "You *are* the chairman of the *chevra kadisha*."

"It's not personal, Jakub. If I could help you, believe me that I would." Offener stood and shook my hand vigorously. "My best to your wife."

I thanked him for his time and hurriedly exited the building. A cold drizzle was falling, plastering damp leaves to the headstones. I had left my umbrella at home, so I had no alternative but to hail a Hansom cab. We cut through the *Kleinseite* and got caught in traffic on the Charles Bridge, which was to be expected, then followed the banks of the Moldau straight to Žižka Square. The driver wished to gossip, but I silenced him with a series of short replies. When we finally arrived at Charlotte Street, it was nearly time for the midday meal.

The door of our flat stood ajar and Lida Rikena was nowhere to be found. But in the center of the sitting room stood the crate labeled PRESERVED MEATS, emitting the musty and faintly noxious odor of long-sealed travelling chests. I found my Ryba in bed, sobbing, accusing Marjeta Samsa of once again ruining her life.

.....

The trouble had begun shortly after I had left for the synagogue, when Lida Rikena learned second-hand from one of the Pastarnack's servant girls what the Samsas' former cook had told her regarding the contents of the wooden crate. Now Lida Rikena had been with us for three years at that time, and the girl was as sweet as a honeycomb, but mightily superstitious. As soon as she discovered that we were harboring the remnants of what she called the "person-roach," she had immediately, and in uncertain terms, informed Ryba that she would not step foot in the apartment again until the offending article was removed. No amount of pleading or cajoling on my wife's part could change her mind. In the end, Ryba had been forced to call off her sewing circle and to postpone the singing lessons she gave the orphaned Marcus twins.

"Come into the kitchen," I begged Ryba, stroking her hair. "We'll have a hearty lunch and we'll talk this through."

"What is there to talk through?" she demanded. "How am I supposed to lead a normal life with an tremendous vermin rotting in my sitting room."

"Please be reasonable, doll." As I said this, I could not help feeling that *I* was the one being unreasonable. "It will only be with us a few days. I'll write to the Jewish cemeteries at Bruenn and Pressburg. . . . We'll ship it to Vienna, if it comes to that."

"I don't *want* to be reasonable. I want you to take that thing down to the curb immediately—let the rats and the beggars make off with it."

"You don't mean that," I pleaded.

"Like hell, I don't mean that," snapped Ryba. "Marjeta Berg lorded it over me for her whole life—and even in poverty and shame, she has once again managed to leave me holding the bag of her crusts and rinds. So let her son rot with the vegetables! What do I care?"

She lurched off the bed suddenly and stormed out of the room. I found her moments later in the sitting room, pounding the makeshift coffin with her tiny fists. Never in my entire memory of our thirty years together had I seen my Ryba so distraught—not even after the miscarriage, not even after Doctor Loesser warned her there could be no children. I grabbed hold of her fragile hands in fear that she might bloody them.

"I'll get rid of it. I promise," I said. "Give me twenty four hours?"

Ryba cupped her palm around her fist and I could sense her struggling for composure.

"Fine. Twenty-four hours," said my wife. "But put a cloth underneath the damn thing because it's starting to ooze. And don't you dare use any of my linens."

.....

Between the *mincha* services and visiting Rabbi Buchmeyer's widow, who had been struck overnight with fever, I walked down to the central post office at *Malé náměstí* and sent person-to-person wires to the directors of the *chevra kadishim* in Bruenn, Pressburg, Vienna and even Cracow. At first, each proved reasonably accommodating. However, once they understood the nature of the deceased's condition, they served up implausible excuses regarding space and customs certification that made their position unmistakably clear. In frustration, I even approached the Lutheran pastor, Hruska, at the church on Leopold Street, as he had a reputation for tolerance and had set himself up against the unvarnished Jew-hating of certain among his Orthodox and Roman Catholic brethren, but the clergyman explained—in deep earnestness—that there was a difference between assisting Jews and assisting dead vermin, and that one had to draw a line somewhere.

Ryba made no mention of the coffin at dinner. She took pains to talk around it—like a physician speaking of the cancer—and a stranger, listening to her speak about an article she'd read on the foods of Palestine and of plans for her niece's engagement feast, might have thought nothing amiss. But I could tell she was counting down the hours, keeping her frustration in check until she could justly demand the removal of the body.

I slept fitfully that night—all I could think of was how ordinary the Samsa boy had seemed, a handsome lad who might have made a good marriage—and I nearly slept through the morning prayers, arriving at the synagogue after the *minyan* had already assembled. All day long, I conjured up ways to dispose of the cadaver, and even contemplated burying it on my own, but the space in the Jewish cemetery was carefully accounted for, and we did not have a yard of our own, so that would mean leaving it in strange and unhallowed ground, where a building crew or a stray animal might easily disturb it. When time came to return home for supper, I still had no plans for the boy's remains, so I sent an errand boy to Charlotte Street with the message that I would be working late. Then I wandered the city through hours twenty-nine, thirty, thirty-one, knowing that every minute I was violating my pledge to Ryba.

When I finally built up the strength to confront her, it was nearly ten o'clock and she was already wearing her sleeping gown. I made no effort to explain my absence, and she made no effort to inquire where I had been. We embraced—as we always did—and she placed my overcoat and on the brass tree in the foyer.

"I am going to bed, Jakub Tzvi," said my wife firmly. "When I wake up in the morning, I expect that . . . monstrosity to be gone. If you can't do that for me after thirty-one years of marriage . . . I don't know what!"

"Please, doll. Let's not end the day with bad feelings between us."

"I don't have any bad feelings," she answered. "Because I know you love me far too much to let that awful thing be here in the morning."

. . . . .

I waited at the dining room table until Ryba had turned off the electric lamp in the bedroom. She was already sleeping like a lamb when I tiptoed into the chamber and kissed her gently on the forehead, careful not to rouse her from her dreams. Then I rummaged through the foyer closet until I found my spare frock coat—part of a stylish wool suit that I had inherited from my father. It was such a finely-tailored garment to discard, but what choice did I have? I quickly retrieved the claw hammer from beneath the sink and pried open the wooden lid of the meat crate. Holding my handkerchief over my mouth and nose, I dropped the coat into the crate and scooped up the contents. Wrapped inside this crude swaddling, the remains felt like a thick, lumpy pudding. One hideous antenna protruded from above the collar of the jacket. In desperation, I immediately removed my own vest and used it to plug up this unfortunate gap in the shroud. When I was certain that that cadaver was not dripping—I didn't want to be the one to trail vermin blood across Ryba's parlor carpet, not to mention the city—I retrieved my top hat and overcoat from the foyer and set out into the night.

The storm clouds had blown away with the twilight, replaced by a bitter chill, and a sharp, clear moonlight now bathed the streets. As the hour was past eleven, there was little likelihood that I might encounter an acquaintance, yet still I walked rapidly and kept to the shadows. Occasionally, a night watchman shined a kerosene torch in my direction—but then merely tipped his cap in courtesy and continued on his patrol. Of far greater concern was the heft of the cadaver, as the Samsa boy had weighed in excess of thirteen stone, and while as a vermin he appeared to be somewhat lighter, he was still quite a challenge for an old man of fifty-eight. By the time I reached the Strasnice District, my forearms had gone numb.

If there was a guard on duty at the New Cemetery, he was not at his post. While the front gates were locked, as I had anticipated, not much effort was required to scale the low perimeter wall on the side farthest from the boulevard, where it met the adjoining hillside at a height of only about four feet. In my haste, I had made no provision for a shovel—I had been far too concerned with keeping the body from leaking—but now fortune smiled upon me, for I found a pair of iron spades in a wheelbarrow beside the *chevra kadisha* offices. I selected the sturdier of the two, although it was smaller.

I also tried on the sheepskin gardening gloves that had been abandoned inside the barrow, but they proved too small for my hands. Then I mustered one final torrent of energy and lugged the corpse into the oldest section of the cemetery. Even in the darkness, I had little difficulty finding the open patch of earth, surrounded by Pollaks and Zeitzes and Smolkovas, which would belong to Ryba and me for eternity. I took one look up at the heavens, where the Great Bear twinkled benightedly, and then I started to dig.

.....

I returned home shortly before daybreak, my trousers caked in dust. The meat crate remained in the sitting room where I had left it, the lid propped against the icebox. I deposited the cover inside the container, without daring to look inside, and carried the foul-smelling box down to the curbside for the rubbish collectors. I am cognizant of the *halakhic* duty to collect even the fragments of a dead man's body for interment—and once combed the concrete myself after the boiler explosion at the glassworks—but I am optimistic that the Lord will forgive me under the strain of the circumstances. The vast majority of Gregor Samsa's remains lay resting safely in my grave, and let us hope that is enough. Where Ryba and I are to be buried—for I am certain my wife will not consent to sharing a plot with her cousin's damaged son—is a quandary whose vast expanse I have only recently begun to fathom.

That night my primary concern was with putting the immediate vestiges of the vermin episode out of sight, so that our lives might return to their usual course. Yet I will confess, passing through the darkened parlor on the way to my marital bed, I was struck with the momentary dread that I would open the bedroom door to find my beloved transformed into a monstrous dung beetle. That did not happen, of course. I found Ryba as I had left her, beautiful and peaceful. She had done nothing to warrant transformation into a vermin—I am certain she was incapable of such a magnitude of sin—and for a moment I convinced myself, watching her delicate breaths, that such a revolting fate was reserved for only those truly worthy.

Jacob M. Appel is a physician, attorney and bioethicist based in New York City. He is the author of more than two hundred published short stories and is a past winner of the Boston Review Short Fiction Competition, the William Faulkner-William Wisdom Award for the Short Story, the Dana Award, the Arts & Letters Prize for Fiction, the *North American Review*'s Kurt Vonnegut Prize, the *Missouri Review*'s Editor's Prize, the *Sycamore Review*'s Wabash Prize, the *Briar Cliff Review*'s Short Fiction Prize, the H. E. Francis Prize, the New Millennium Writings Fiction Award in four different years, an Elizabeth George Fellowship and a Sherwood Anderson Foundation Writers Grant. His stories have been short-listed for the O. Henry Award, *Best American Short Stories*, *Best American Nonrequired Reading*, *Best American Mystery Stories*, and the Pushcart Prize anthology on numerous occasions. His first novel, *The Man Who Wouldn't Stand Up*, won the Dundee International Book Prize in 2012. Jacob holds graduate degrees from Brown University, Columbia University's College of Physicians and Surgeons, Harvard Law School, New York University's MFA program in fiction and Albany Medical College's Alden March Institute of Bioethics. He taught for many years at Brown University and currently teaches at the Gotham Writers' Workshop and the Mount Sinai School of Medicine.